Hilary

Hilary

by

Jerry B. Jenkins

MOODY PRESS

CHICAGO

To Wally Kroeker

©1980 by
Jerry B. Jenkins

Library of Congress Cataloging in Publication Data

Jenkins, Jerry B
  Hilary.

  I. Title.
PS3560.E485H5   813'.54   80-20256
ISBN 0-8024-4313-3

Printed in the United States of America

A Synopsis of *Margo* (Book No. 1)

Philip Spence, a free-lance artist from Dayton, Ohio, is returning to the elevator after a business meeting in an Atlanta skyscraper when he happens upon Margo Franklin, apparently contemplating suicide at a thirtieth-floor window.

Her father is a wealthy garment industry executive, and her mother is a circuit judge in the criminal courts of Cook County in Chicago. Margo's parents, who raised her in the fashionable and exclusive North Shore suburb of Winnetka, have long since divorced. What has pushed Margo to the brink of suicide is that her mother is trying a man for a murder that Margo believes was committed by her mother, Judge Franklin herself.

Philip convinces Margo that she should expose her mother and then agrees to help her. During the ordeal, Philip shares with Margo his rusty faith in Christ. After a long process of reading many things Philip offers, and wondering just what it was in Philip that made him care so much about a stranger, Margo receives Christ.

The case against Mrs. Franklin brings Margo and Philip to Chicago under the protection of Earl Haymeyer, a special agent for the United States attorney's office in charge of the investigation. Philip and Margo grow close, and they become friends with Haymeyer.

Mrs. Franklin stonewalls it to the end, trying to implicate her former husband in the murder. When his alibi proves invulnerable, the United States attorney arranges a meeting with Mrs. Franklin, Margo, Philip, Haymeyer, and Mrs. Franklin's attorney, Amos Chakaris.

Mrs. Franklin at first tries to shift the blame for the murder to Margo, but her defense crumbles and in an emotional scene she finally admits her guilt. In Philip's account at the end of the book, Mrs. Franklin addresses Margo in that final scene:

"Sure you've been hurt, but look at what I've been through. What do I have left? I know I'm grabbing at thin air, but air is all I've got. Now you stand here and tell me I'm not what I used to be. That I'm killing you by being this way. Well, I ask you, what am I supposed to be like? What is the dignified thing to do now?"

Margo stared at her mother. "I want you to accept my forgiveness."

Virginia Franklin's face was contorted. She shook her head. "You can't forgive me," she said. "You simply cannot. I won't let you. It's impossible."

"You don't *want* my forgiveness?"

"What will it do for me? Your forgiveness would belittle me—crush me. I would be humiliated even more, if that's possible."

"But I offer love."

"Margo, you're loving my memory. You can't love me now."

"I can and I do."

"You can't love me!"

"God is loving you through me." Margo's tears flowed freely now. "I hate the things you do, and I pity you. But God lets me love you in spite of myself."

Mrs. Franklin broke down. I thought I'd never see her cry. "Margo, Margo," she said. "What should I do?"

Margo embraced her. "Give it up, Mother. Just give it up."

"I'll suffer. I'll pay. You know I'll be sentenced. And I'll be alone."

Margo held her closer. "You'll never be alone. God loves you, Mother. I love you. You'll always have me."

And Margo would always have me.

A Synopsis of *Karlyn* (Book No. 2)

Philip hopes a painful chapter in his life will end with the sentencing of Virginia Franklin to the women's facility at the Illinois State Prison in Pontiac, but things hardly settle down for him before Margo decides to move to Pontiac to be close to her mother.

Earl Haymeyer talks Philip into giving up full-time free-lancing as an artist and moving to Glencoe, Illinois, to join him in his new venture, the "EH Detective Agency / Private Investigations." With Margo close to landing a job in Pontiac and soon to be able to visit her mother at the prison for the first time, Philip loses himself in his first assignment for Earl.

By the time the puzzling Karlyn May case is solved, Philip and Margo have come to independent decisions that they should no longer be apart. Near the end of the book, Philip calls Margo in Pontiac:

"I want you to come up here between now and when you have to start your job," I said. "I can't take anymore."

"That's good to hear," she said. "I'm bored to death here with nothing to do, and there's a lot I want to talk about. Living this far apart just isn't going to make it."

"My sentiments exactly."

I felt for Margo and all that she had been through. It was unfair that so much of her life had been eaten up by the problems with her mother. And now those apron strings had reached right out of the prison walls and ensnared her again.

When I saw her again, I would tell her all that I had been thinking about. . . . If I could somehow express to her all that she meant to me and how much I loved her and needed her, perhaps we could work out something more equitable than living a couple of hundred miles apart. Especially if we were married. That is, if she would say yes. . . . When Margo arrives, Philip asks:

"Got any plans for lunch?"

"Hardly."

"Keep your coat on."

Chapter One

If I hadn't let Margo speak first, we'd be engaged now.

Earl had told me about a charming little place for lunch just north of the Loop. Margo sat close in the car and lay her head on my shoulder. "I have so much to talk to you about," she said quietly.

"Me too," I said.

"But me first. How much time do we have?"

"Unless you've accepted a job you have to run back to Pontiac for, we have the rest of the day. Earl gave me the afternoon off."

"Any more cases coming up?"

"Oh, I'm sure. Earl got started on several while I was concentrating on Karlyn—on her case, I mean. We'll be starting in on something the first thing tomorrow morning."

At the restaurant I held her hands across the table. The moment was perfect for my big question, but I had promised to let her speak first. "I don't want to be away from you anymore," she said quickly.

So she was going to make it easy for me. "Me either,"

I said, my courage building. She put a finger to my mouth.

"I want to forget about Pontiac, move up here, get an apartment, and get a job that really excites me."

"What excites me is the thought of your being so close," I said. "Then we could—"

She quieted me again. "I can visit Mother once a week. It will be difficult and expensive, but I can see her only once a week anyway. I find myself coming up here to see you more often than that, and I can see you anytime."

"How would you like to see me every day for the rest of your life?"

She ignored me. "I suppose you're wondering how this all came about and what Mother might think of it."

"Uh, yeah, OK."

"Well, her last two letters—I can see her in three days, by the way—have been so insistent about my not staying in Pontiac but finding myself a career, that she has nearly convinced me. I still want to see her whenever I can, but every lonely night I spend down there confirms all the more that I need to move on, to grow. To grow *up*."

"What do you want to do?" I asked.

"I want to do what you do."

I raised my eyebrows. Maybe the Karlyn May case had intrigued her, but there had been a lot of drudgery in it that she wouldn't have known about. What if she lost interest? And a woman in detective work? I was enough of a chauvinist to think twice about it. I smiled at her, not knowing what to say.

10

"I know what you're thinking, Sherlock," she said. "Afraid of the competition?"

I laughed. "What will it mean to our future?" I said. "I want to marry you."

The waitress brought our salads and we prayed silently. Margo looked at me, but I couldn't read her thoughts. "I've been thinking a lot about that too, Philip."

"And?"

"And I want time."

"Time for what? We've been together constantly for months, up until the last few weeks."

"I want to get to know you as a normal person, not as one who pitied me, or who led me to Christ, or who protected and helped me."

"I don't pity you—"

"Anymore."

"OK, anymore, but I do want to protect you and help you and whatever else goes along with loving you."

"But don't you see that there hasn't been a normal day in our relationship?"

"And you think there will be if you become a private investigator too?"

"The attention will be focused on someone else's problems, not mine. We've been so wrapped up in my problems that we haven't had a chance to breathe."

Margo had always been hard to argue with. "So what does it mean to our future?" I repeated.

"It means we'll get to know each other well. If you're still convinced in a few months that I am what you want, let's talk about it then."

11

"How come you make everything sound so cut and dried and businesslike? And how about you? Do you still have to be convinced that I'm what you want?"

"No."

"But if I asked you right now to marry me, you'd make me wait so *you* would be sure that *I* was sure?"

"You got it."

"Grief."

I was genuinely irritated, but I wasn't sure why. I couldn't blame her for wanting me to be sure, but I was insulted that she thought I didn't know my own mind. I pouted a while, but she ignored it. We ate in silence.

"You don't just *become* a private investigator," Earl Haymeyer said in his Glencoe office late that afternoon.

"Why not?" Margo challenged. "Philip did."

"No, Philip didn't. To get him his license, I had to verify that he had been personally involved in many of the investigations that led to your mother's arrest. I also had to pledge that he would be properly trained in the use of firearms before he is allowed to carry a gun, and that I would enroll him in an accredited six-week course on crime detection and prevention as soon as an opening arises. Your three-day qualifying screener begins tomorrow, Philip."

I was surprised.

"I just got the call a little while ago," Earl explained. He turned back to Margo. "If you think this business is fun, or you just want to try it as a lark, I don't encourage it."

"You know me better than that, Earl," Margo said. "I

really want to do it. Maybe someday Philip and I will work as a team."

"That'll do wonders for your marriage," Earl said. "Anyway, where do you think you're going to work? There's not a detective agency I know of that would take a chance on a totally inexperienced young woman with no training, and, for all anyone knows, no aptitude for the work. Jobs are scarce and money is tight."

"You could teach me, Earl. Just like you're teaching Philip. In fact, Philip could teach me secondhand."

"There's no way," Earl said. "I've had a dozen cases dropped in my lap from old acquaintances. I won't even be able to train Philip the way I want to. That's why I'm glad this opening at training school came for Philip. It usually takes months to even get into a screening class."

"That just proves you need help, Earl," Margo persisted. "And that you'll have the money to hire more people."

"You're hopeless, Margo," Earl said. "I just can't encourage you, as much as I'd like to."

"How would you like it if I landed with some other agency? I will, you know."

"You probably would," Earl said. "I'll tell you what I'll do: I'll let you work in the office, and I'll put your name on the waiting list for a screening class."

"I don't want to be a secretary."

"You may be here for a while. I've just converted from a temporary to a full-time girl, and she could use some help. You could pick up a lot about the business by being in the office until we hear about your application."

"I suppose that would be all right. I really don't have

13

a choice unless I want to take some other kind of a job in the meantime. And I am moving up here, job or not."

"I don't want you getting any false hopes, though," Earl said. "We were lucky to get Philip into a screener class as early as we did, and he had a lot going for him."

"Like what?"

I looked at Margo.

"I mean, what did he have going for him?" she said, trying to improve on her question.

"A little experience, a couple of well-placed references, things like that."

"Which I wouldn't have?"

"All you'd have on your resume is that you help out in our offices. The fact that you are a woman will not help you, as illegal as any discrimination might be. You should know that any law can be circumvented if every angle is studied enough. They could drub you out because of your sex and blame it on any number of other reasons."

"You're not very optimistic."

"I'm glad you're getting the point, Margo. The worst part is, you could get into a screening class and then fail to qualify for the six-week course, which follows a month or so later."

"The same could happen for Philip."

"Sure it could, but he doesn't have any natural barriers to overcome. And he does have some background now."

"Are you offering me a job in the meantime?"

"If you're willing to do clerical work, not grumble about it, keep your ears open, and accept an appropriate salary. I don't want you around here just biding your time, because your time may never come."

"Thank you, Dale Carnegie," Margo said.

That evening Margo showed me the letters she had received from her mother. They troubled me. They evidenced all the predictable bitterness of a woman who had been to the heights of power as a judge, now reduced to a denim-wearing number in a facility full of hard women. But there was more.

She complained of dizziness, lack of orientation, listlessness. She said she thought it was the "lousy chicken they seem to feed me every meal in my cell." Margo thought it was her mother's veiled request for the earliest possible visit allowed by law. I was left simply shaken by it.

For one thing, I wasn't aware that she was segregated from the other prisoners even for meals. And of all the things I expected from tough, old Virginia Franklin, physical problems were not among them.

One of the letters even told of an overnight stay in the infirmary. "That doesn't sound like your mother," I said.

"Oh, she's all right," Margo said. "She may be seeking a little sympathy. I'll find out when I see her."

"When is that again?"

"Three days from now. And I'd like you to go with me."

"We'll see. My qualifying class will be over, so maybe I can take a day."

Chapter Two

For the next three days I endured a battery of tests to determine if I had the psychological and physical aptitude to study crime detection and prevention. The tests were fascinating lessons in themselves. At the end of each day I drove back to suburban Glencoe for dinner with Margo, who had a ton of questions.

"You know there are a lot of things I can't tell you because we are sworn to secrecy," I said. "They remind us often that there are many people who plan to take the tests and would pay anything for an idea of what they contain."

"OK, what's your price?" she teased.

"I ought to report this attempted bribe."

Earl gave me permission to drive Margo back down to Pontiac and help her move north if I agreed to be back to work two days later. I was so keyed up over the tests that I would have been good for nothing to him anyway.

"How do you think you did?" Earl wanted to know.

"It's hard to say. Some of the questions seemed so ridiculously easy that I may have missed something. Others were Greek to me."

"That's the way it seemed to me years ago," Earl admitted. "And I was allowed into the class."

All the way to Pontiac, Margo tried to assure me that she knew what she was doing, and that if I thought about it carefully, I'd realize that her main motivation for moving to the Chicago area was to be near me. I believed her, but she couldn't hide the excitement in her voice when she talked of getting into detective work. That opportunity had a lot to do with her decision too.

When we arrived at her place, letters were waiting for her from both her mother and father. She opened the one from her father first. Shortly after her mother's trial, Mr. Franklin had moved to California to become a garment industry consultant. Now he told Margo of "a wonderful woman" he had met. "She's also a transplanted Chicagoan," he reported. "We've not dated long, but something tells me you might have a reason to visit me out here very soon."

"I can't believe it," Margo said. "He hardly ever saw any other women after Mother divorced him. Now he sounds ready to get married again after all this time."

"How does it make you feel?"

"Protective, I guess. I want to know who she is, what her intentions are, all that." Margo laughed at herself. "Listen to me," she said.

She opened the letter from her mother. "Perhaps by the time you read this I'll have already seen you. And that means I will have talked you into leaving Pontiac and following your head and heart to Philip and a career. That's what I want for you."

18

"She's in the infirmary again," Margo said flatly. "I don't guess I like that too much. Still complaining about the poultry not agreeing with her. I'm afraid she's just used to gourmet food."

I asked to see the letter. The rest had the usual complaints of a woman out of her element. No one listened to her or understood when they did listen. "It will be good to talk to you soon," she wrote, "just to have someone half intelligent to banter with. And yes, you may hit me once again with your Christian ideas, if you promise not to take more than half our time together with it."

"That should encourage you," I said.

"Sort of," Margo said.

I could tell the news of the infirmary was troubling her. Her mother wrote nothing of exactly why she was there.

"I'm going to call," Margo said.

I followed her to the hall phone. She dialed the prison. "I don't know who to ask for," Margo began. "I have a relative who's an inmate, and I know I can't talk to her . . . yes, in the women's facility. Thank you." She waited. "Hello, I don't know who to talk to, but I have a relative who's an inmate there . . . yes, a woman. . . . No, I don't know her number." Margo shuddered. "Virginia Frank—yes, that's right." Margo covered the mouthpiece and whispered, "I guess they all know who she is.

"Yes, I know she's in the infirmary and that I can't see her yet, but—oh, I can? Yes, if that's OK." She turned to me again. "They drop the visit and call restrictions when an inmate is in the infirmary. Hello? Mother? Oh, I'm sorry. I was told I could talk to her. Well, could you tell me what's wrong with her? . . . How can I prove I'm her daughter without coming there? I'm due there tomorrow, but I'd come tonight if I could get some information. . . . I see. OK, thank you, nurse. . . . I'm sorry, doctor. I'll see you tomorrow."

Margo was upset. "She's sleeping now. I could have seen her a few days ago when she was put in the infirmary for the second time. She probably didn't even know that. They never told me. The doctor won't tell me anything by phone, and I can't get in there this late. I'll be anxious to see Mother tomorrow. And the doctor too."

I stayed at the local TraveLodge that night and met Margo at about nine the next morning. We could not visit her mother until ten, so we ate quickly and just drove around, trying to ease the tension. "I've got so much to tell her," Margo said. "She'll be glad to hear of my plans. At least I hope she'll be. Maybe down deep she really wants me to stay near her."

I let her ramble. In a strange way, I was anxious to see Mrs. Franklin again myself. We agreed that I would just greet her, talk a few minutes, and then leave while Margo looked for the right opportunity to talk to her again about God.

"One of these times we're going to get through to her," Margo predicted. "I just know it. The Bible says that God will give you the desires of your heart, and that's my desire. Can there by anything selfish about that desire, Philip?"

I thought for a moment. "Not that I can see."

"I know she was wrong," Margo said. "But she's long overdue for some peace and forgiveness."

"You already forgave her," I said.

"And God will too," she said, "but somehow she can't see that. I want to hook up with the chaplain here and start really working on Mother."

"Ganging up on her might not be the answer," I said. "Persistence is the key. The right time will come. It will all hit her at once, and she will be most moved by the fact that you cared enough to stay by her."

"I don't know if I ever prayed for anything so hard in my life."

"I know what you mean," I said.

"No, you don't. But thanks anyway."

The main receiving room looked less like a prison than the outside walls and gates did, yet that same cold formality permeated the place. Neither of us had been there before, of course, so we tentatively followed the signs to an information desk. Margo clutched my arm so tightly that I knew she wanted me to get us into the infirmary.

"We're here to see Virginia Franklin," I said.

"Your names, please."

"Philip Spence and Margo Fr—"

"There is someone here to see you, sir," the guard said.

"Pardon me?" I said. Margo stiffened. Then I saw Earl. And Amos Chakaris, the huge, aged lawyer who had represented Mrs. Franklin at the trial. My first impulse was to smile. "What are you guys doing here?" I asked, a little too loudly and much too cheerfully.

"Let's go in here," Haymeyer said, nodding toward an anteroom with heavy wood furnishings. I started to fall in behind the two men, but Margo hardly moved, holding me back. Her eyes were fiery. She wanted answers before she went anywhere.

"What *are* you two doing here, Earl?" she demanded, her voice echoing through the hall and turning the heads of other visitors.

Chakaris and Haymeyer looked at each other soberly for an instant and then at me. I was still puzzled. Margo wasn't. She knew they had news she didn't want to hear. "Please," Earl said, putting his hands on her shoulders and guiding her, stiff-legged, into the room.

"Please sit down, honey," Chakaris said, helping Haymeyer ease her into a straight-backed chair. Margo looked as if she wanted them to get to it. Her eyes were already filling. I sat dumbfounded.

Chakaris slid a tissue box across the table in front of Margo. She stared at Earl. "Your mother died early this morning, Margo," he said. She shook her head. "She was run down from a cold, and she wasn't adjusting. She didn't respond to medication and when she developed heart trouble, she had no reserves. She was gone quickly."

Margo closed her eyes and drew her fists up before her face. She trembled until her entire body shook. I moved to comfort her but was no help. She interlocked her fingers and pressed her lips against her hands. Still she shivered.

Amos started to say that it might have been for the best because she was so miserable in this place, but I signaled him to silence, knowing that Margo was probably preoccupied with the fact that her mother was much worse off now than she had been during her first few weeks in prison.

Haymeyer and Chakaris paced the room, not looking at Margo and occasionally staring out the window. "Do you want us to leave?" Earl asked. Margo shook her head.

"Do you want anything?" I asked.

She didn't respond.

"How long can we stay here?" I whispered to Earl. He shrugged. "Let's just give her some time then," I said. "And then we can take her home."

"Would you like to see her?" Chakaris asked softly. Margo nodded.

"I'll see what I can do," he said, and left.

"I don't understand," Margo said weakly. "Mother never wrote anything about having a cold."

Earl tried to explain again about how the combination of shocks to her mental and physical health had sneaked up on her, but Margo made a face and he fell silent.

Chakaris returned. Margo looked at him expectantly. He nodded. "When you feel you're ready."

"Can Philip go with me?"

"Of course."

Margo tried to stand, then sat again. "I guess I'm not ready," she said.

"There's no rush," Chakaris said. "The coroner is here because autopsies are mandatory in prison deaths before the bodies can be moved. I will see that she is transported back to Chicago for you, if you wish."

"Amos," Margo whined, "I don't know anything about this or what I should do—"

The old man raised both hands to silence her. "Shhh," he said. "You know I have always represented your mother. I have all her important documents and am executor of her will. She has stipulated where she is to be taken, what kind of service she wants, everything. I'll handle it. OK?"

Margo nodded gratefully and stood. As we moved slowly down the hall, Margo leaning heavily on me, Amos told Earl that the regular Pontiac coroner was not there. "This guy is from up north," he said. "I didn't even know he served the Department of Corrections."

Chapter Three

Margo controlled herself during one last look at her mother's body, but as Mrs. Franklin was wheeled away, Margo broke down.

With Earl and Amos's help, we had Margo packed and ready to move to Chicago in less than an hour. She wanted to help, and we probably should have let her, but we insisted that she just sit and wait for us, as if grief and shock were exhausting. Later she admitted that they were.

During the drive north, Margo was mostly silent. And angry. "I don't want any of your platitudes," she said when I tried to console her. And I couldn't deny that trying to explain the good purpose of such a death was beyond me. In a way, her lashing out at me saved me some awkward moments; anything I might have thought to say seemed hollow when I even considered it.

"I'll be praying for you," I said weakly.

"Yes, I suppose you will," she said. "Why don't you just try holding me for now?"

I drove with one arm around her, traveling slower than usual, as if hitting a bump or swerving would injure her. After a long silence, she said, "I've got to call Daddy."

"Now?"

She shook her head. "When we get back."

"I wish I knew what to say to you," I admitted.

"Just ignore me for a few days, will you?"

"How can I, Margo? You don't really want me to, do you?"

"I mean ignore what I say. I'm not handling this well, and I don't know what I might say. I might even hurt you, Philip. And I probably already have." She was right. "But I need you to bear with me, to love me, to not give up on me."

"I would never give up on you, Margo."

"Not even if I said I thought God had made a mistake and that I might not forgive Him?"

"You don't know what you're saying."

"Of course I don't; that's what I just said!"

"It's not our pl—"

"Don't tell me it's not my place to forgive God or not forgive Him! I know all that! Please, Philip, don't preach at me now. Just let me be."

"Just let you be what? Angry at God?"

She didn't answer.

Earl opened an apartment for Margo in his building, not far from mine. "I'll want to get a place somewhere else as soon as possible, Earl," she said. "Philip and I don't need this kind of pressure. But I do appreciate it more than you know."

She called her father from Earl's office. "He's coming on the next plane," she reported.

"How'd he take it?"

"I couldn't tell. He sounded pretty stunned. He asked if he could bring his fiancee."

"And?"

"I've quit telling Daddy what to do. It's always been too easy, and it was what Mother did for so long. He needs to make his own decisions. I think it would be tacky to show up with a fiancee at his former wife's funeral, but it also makes sense to have her come along so I can meet her."

"So is he bringing her?"

"He didn't say."

Bonnie, Earl's new secretary, a matronly, fiftyish woman, silently took in our conversation, then stood and approached. She took Margo's hands in hers. "We've never met," she said. "But I feel I know you. I followed the story of your mother in the papers, and Earl has told me so much about you. I just want you to know how badly I feel about this and that I would do anything at all if there's any way I can help."

Margo looked at her incredulously, as if she could hardly believe that a stranger could be so kind. She couldn't speak. She fell into Bonnie's arms and cried loudly. The phone rang, but Bonnie didn't even make a move for it. She asked with her eyes if I would answer it.

"EH Detective Agency," I said.

"Yeah, uh, Mr. Haymeyer?"

"No, this is Philip Spence. Can I—"

"Oh, good, Philip, it's you. This is George Franklin, but please don't let on that it's me if Margo is there."

"Oh, OK, sir. How are you? It's been a long time."

"I'm OK, Philip. Listen, let me tell you something

27

straight here. Gladys, my fiancee, she's not real hot about my coming back there for this funeral. You understand?"

"I think so. Does that mean you're not, I mean, what does that mean?"

"Right, Philip. I'm not going to be able to make it, but I'd appreciate it if you'd tell Margo another reason, like maybe this threatened air traffic controllers' strike everyone's talking about. Tell her I'm afraid I'll get stranded in Chicago or something, and with the new business, you know I can't afford that."

"OK, is that all? Are you sure you don't want to talk to—"

"No, I'd appreciate it if you'd handle that for me, Philip."

I knew Mr. Franklin wanted to come. He had loved Mrs. Franklin for years after the divorce and was especially supportive of her during the trial, though she resisted all his help. Everyone knew he posted the exhorbitant bond so she was free until her sentencing, but she had never thanked him. Still, he would have come. It was now more of the same for George Franklin. A woman was trying to make a man out of him by making him do what she said.

I didn't care if I ever met Gladys.

"Daddy will be calling back with his flight number, Bonnie," Margo said. "Just let me know, and I'll pick him up at the airport. Philip, will you go with me?"

"Your father just called and told me to tell you that he's afraid of getting stranded in Chicago if this

28

threatened air traffic controllers' strike comes off. He's not coming."

"Of course he is; let me call him again."

"Margo," I said, as gently as I could, "if he had wanted to talk to you, he could have."

She glared at me. "What are you saying?"

"That he didn't want to disappoint you, but he is not coming, and your calling him is not going to change anything."

Margo sat at Bonnie's desk, refusing to cry again. I hung around, not knowing what to say or do. I wanted to criticize her father and tell her the real reason, but it would not have helped. "You don't have to stay with me all the time, you know, Philip," she said.

"It's no bother," I said.

"Yes," she said. "It is."

I got the point and left. Later Bonnie called me in my apartment. "When my husband died a few years ago," she said, "I didn't want my closest loved ones to hover. I wanted them there, or not too far away, but I didn't want them uncomfortable. You looked uncomfortable. Like you were pitying her."

"Well, I *am* pitying her."

"Of course, Philip. We all are. We just need to be whatever she needs us to be right now. For you that means to take charge. Don't wait for things to happen. Make them happen. Don't try to console her; just tell her what happens next and see that it happens. I'm going to talk Margo into staying at my place tonight. It's not far away, and I think she needs to just get away right now.

"But listen, Philip, when it's time for the funeral or

meetings with the lawyers or whatever, just take charge. Tell her you're coming for her and then do it. I think she's reacting a little toward her dad, who doesn't sound like a strong man."

"If you only knew," I said. "Thanks for everything, Bonnie."

Amos Chakaris told me at dinner that night that Mrs. Franklin's will requested that only a few close friends attend an interfaith-style service and burial within twenty-four hours of her death. "Which is nearly impossible in this state because of the autopsy, but I think we can make it within thirty hours."

"And who suffers if you don't?" I said.

"Well, Philip," he said, "I understand what you're saying, but where I come from—or maybe I should say, at my age—we have real respect for the dead and for their predeath wishes. I'll feel much better if we do all we can to grant those wishes."

"What other wishes were there?"

"Most everything else simply involves disposing of the estate. I'm not really at liberty to discuss the details until it has been read to the principals, or in this case, the principal—Margo."

"Can I be there for that?"

"It's entirely up to her."

Chakaris and Virginia Franklin went back a long way. He spent much of the rest of the evening recounting the days when she had been the crackerjack prosecutor and he was one of her toughest rivals. "She was always the consummate professional with the highest standards.

Nothing dirty, nothing underhanded, nothing personal. We respected and admired each other until the end."

"You admired her even after you found out she murdered Richard Wanmacher?"

"No. To me that *was* the end. I don't know how or why she happened to take that turn, but I do know it was a turn. When I knew her best, she was straight, unimpeachable, above reproach. Seeing her fall was one of the most painful things I have ever been through. In my mind, her death is the kindest thing that has happened to her since she decided to kill a man."

Chakaris said that the autopsy report bore out the infirmary doctor's evaluation of the cause of death and filled me in on the funeral details. He said he had been given the power to invite up to ten people—based on his knowledge of the deceased—whom he thought she would want there. He had decided upon former United States Attorney James A. Hanlon, Earl Haymeyer, myself, Margo, and Mr. Franklin. "Of course, Margo can bring whoever she wants, also."

I explained Mr. Franklin's plight—to Chakaris's puzzlement—and asked if Mrs. Franklin didn't have any other friends.

"Are you kidding? The woman abandoned most of her social, business, and civic contacts during the last several years. I hardly spoke to her for two years before she called me one night and asked me to represent her before Jim Hanlon.

"Any friends she might have had in the Cook County circuit courts have dropped her like a hot potato since the mob ties and the murder were revealed. Even people who pity her would not want to be seen at her funeral."

"So it will be a mighty small gathering," I said.

"For sure," Chakaris said wearily. "Tomorrow morning at ten at the interfaith chapel in Kenilworth."

I called Bonnie's place at about ten that night and asked if Margo was sleeping. "Not really," Bonnie said, "and she did want me to wake her if you called. Now remember what I said."

"Yes, ma'am," I said, with mock deference.

I told Margo I would pick her up at nine the next morning for the funeral and that Amos had said she could bring anyone she wanted. "Even Bonnie?" she asked.

"Sure, if she wants to come." She did. "How are you doing, love?"

"I'm OK, Philip. I owe you a lot of apologies, I know, but for now, I'm OK."

"You owe me nothing. I'll see you at nine."

"You're sweet. 'Bye."

Chapter Four

Even with me on one side of her and Bonnie on the other, Margo didn't do too well at the funeral. The service was predictably antiseptic, no mention made of any turmoil whatever in Mrs. Franklin's life, let alone that she had served time for murder. Nothing was said even of her contribution to society as a lawyer or judge. We could have been burying anyone, and indeed we were. We were listening to a canned funeral service that, but for the filling in of "her" for "him" and "Virginia Franklin" for "John Doe," was the same service held there nearly every day.

That didn't help Margo, and neither did the absence of her father. "I feel like an orphan," she said at one point. There was nothing I could say. I wanted to be her mother and father and lover and friend. When the "interfaith" clergyman said, "Virginia is now resting in the peace that is her reward," I feared Margo would be sick.

She was silent and shaky as we left the cemetery. Amos strode up and told her that he would read the will for her and for anyone else that she wanted present, "whenever you wish."

"The sooner the better," she said. "Can we do it this week?"

"If you're sure that's what you want," he said. "Would you rather wait?"

"No. I want to put all this behind me as soon as I can."

Amos agreed to call her later with a specific date and time. "Wait until you see *his* offices," Margo told me incongruously.

Several nights later I saw what she meant. Not far from Chicago's Loop, the three floors of a turn-of-the-century mansion had been refurbished to accommodate the prestigious law firm of Chakaris, Fenton, Henley, and Whitehead and its twenty-eight lawyers.

The will was to be read at 9:00 P.M., and I was amazed that so many of the staff were still at the office. Chakaris himself answered the mystery when he arrived. "Good question, Philip. Though our staff is among the best and most dedicated in this city, nine o'clock is a little late for this many to still be here. They're here because I'm here.

"You see, the bigger and older a firm becomes, the more legendary its partners become. We seldom rub shoulders with the staff much anymore, so if they get so much as a chance to greet one of us, they take it. And if they can impress us by simply being here late at night when they know we're in, so much the better."

"Does it work?"

"Oh, a little. I did the same thing when I was young, tried to look busy when the big boss came in. What they don't realize is that we are often in here late at night on

34

unscheduled business they wouldn't know about. Fewer 'selfless' staffers are here then, I can tell you."

"How would all these people know you were going to be in tonight?"

"Oh, you'd be surprised how quickly word travels around here. Law offices are great for rumors and grapevines. Usually accurate, too. But I wouldn't kid myself that all these people are here on my account. The other partners have just as many impressionable staffers as I do. They're going to be here tonight too."

"Your three partners? The names I saw on the plate outside?"

"Right. At ten o'clock I'm giving up my semiretired role in the company. It will be the first change of names in the company in more than thirty years. I'm the original owner, and I took on Hollis Fenton more than forty years ago. A few years later we promoted Thomas Henley, then Clarence Whitehead. It's been Chakaris, Fenton, Henley, and Whitehead ever since."

"So this is a major move."

"You bet. Even though I semiretired a couple of years ago—with a party and the whole bit—I've remained active a couple of days a week. Now I'll be out, though I assume the boys will want to keep my name on the door and the stationery."

"So why is this such a big deal, making official what has been in the works for two years?"

"Philip, my boy, there will be fireworks tonight. Any time a partner leaves the firm, the other partners jockey for position."

"Isn't it automatic? I mean if they move your name

from first to last in the lineup, don't the other three just move up in order?"

"Often yes, but that wouldn't cause the fireworks I predicted, would it?"

"No."

"Confidentially, one of the big boys is going to find himself out of the usual lineup, and possibly even voted out of a partnership."

"Can that be done?"

"It's complicated, but our firm is set up in such a way that the majority rules in a vote of the partners. That means no partner had better be alone on a vote, or he loses. If he can get one other vote, a tie forestalls any changes."

"Who's in trouble?"

"I can't tell you that. But I can tell you that my official resignation becomes effective before the vote on the order of the names, so I will not be a voting member."

"Is that significant?"

"Only because it allows me to sit back and watch. I would be concerned if the very minute I was out the boys voted someone in or out and changed the face of the business in a way I disapproved of. But that is their right."

"Is that what they'll be doing tonight, taking advantage of the fact that you have no vote?"

"No, Philip. If I was voting tonight, I would be voting with the majority."

A phone message came for Chakaris. Margo and I sat in silence. I was fascinated by the workings of this office and the power the partners seemed to have, but it was obvious that Margo could not concentrate on it. This would be an ordeal for her, and she simply wanted it over with.

"Don't take this wrong, Margo," I said, "but what do you think you will be left from your mother's estate?"

"I don't know. Some of the stuff from the house, I suppose. Daddy will get the house. I mean it's his anyway."

"How can that be? Didn't she win it in the divorce settlement years ago?"

"I guess. All I know is that he always made the payments on it. Still does, I think. I wouldn't know how much it's worth by now. They bought it more than twenty years ago, but for how much, I don't know."

A court reporter came in with his equipment in tow, informed the secretary of his presence, and sat next to us on a leather couch. "Big doings here tonight, huh?" he said. "This many people here to hear the Franklin will?"

Margo shrugged.

"Not really," I said. "Most are just staffers here."

"Oh," he said, taking in the dark wood trim and beautiful furnishings. "A meeting of the partners tonight, then?"

"How'd you know?"

"Either everyone on this staff has a trial tomorrow morning, or something's going on."

Chakaris's secretary motioned for the court reporter to come upstairs. "You may come along in about five minutes too," she told us. For some reason, I was nervous.

37

As we started up the stairs, a distinguished man in his mid-sixties came down as if each step was a surprise. "Good evening," he said with a slight bow. "You must be Philip and Margo. Charmed. I'm Hollis Fenton. So nice to meet you."

He was so smooth he nearly overwhelmed us. We were speechless. "Amos asked if I would introduce you to the lawyer who will be handling any of the detail work of the Franklin estate subsequent to the reading of the will."

"We'd be happy to meet him," I said.

"*Her*," Fenton corrected, a sliver of ice in his tone.

He led us upstairs to the door of the room in which the will would be read. From another wing came a young woman in her mid-twenties, tweed clad, nearly six feet tall, with long, black hair, huge eyes, and an incredible face. I stared and Margo noticed, almost amused.

"This," said Fenton with a flourish, "is Miss Hilary Brice, attorney at law. She will be—"

"Thank you very much, Mr. Fenton," Hilary said, turning her back on him and motioning to us with a thin attaché. "Will you follow me, please?"

Fenton was left broiling in the hall as Hilary closed the door. "Philip and Margo," she said, "I trust that the reading of the will would be the end of the legal association between you and our firm, but if not, I will be handling anything for Mr. Chakaris, who is retiring shortly."

She was crisp and to the point and, except for the quite obvious brush-off of Hollis Fenton, seemed pleasant and even a little shy. She certainly knew what to say and when to say it. I pictured Mr. Fenton in the hallway, plotting her demise. How could a young lawyer do a number like that on a man who had been a partner in the firm for forty years?

Amos sat at one end of a long wooden table, and the court reporter—already entering script—listened as Amos monotoned preliminary file numbers. "Are we all here?" he asked, looking up. I nodded as if I knew, then realized that I didn't.

"I believe so, yes," Hilary said.

"Off the record," Amos said, glancing at the reporter, "Margo, I am pleased to tell you before I read this aloud that you are about to become an extremely wealthy young woman."

Margo was nonplussed. She shot a double take at Chakaris and then at me. Hilary overruled a grin. "Get on with it, counselor," she said.

"Let the record show who is present," Chakaris began. "Amos Chakaris, senior partner in the firm of Chakaris, Fenton, Henley, and Whitehead, in his final official duty for the same—"

"Excuse me, sir," the court reporter interrupted, "but do you want all that on the record?"

"Do you mind?" Chakaris asked Margo. "This is, after all, really recorded for you."

"Oh, not at all," Margo said. "As long as you're not going to recount your entire legal history just for the books."

Everyone laughed. Chakaris continued: "Also Margo Franklin, daughter of the deceased—" That sobered Margo again. "—Philip Spence of Glencoe, Illinois, and the youngest and most beautiful junior partner this law firm has ever had, Hilary Brice."

The court reporter hesitated, Hilary pursed her lips and shook her head, and Chakaris resignedly said, "Strike that. There might have been one younger."

This time Margo was not amused, and Chakaris noticed. He quickly began the laborious reading into the record all the legal jargon:

"I, Virginia A. Franklin, of Winnetka, Illinois, being of sound and disposing mind and memory, do hereby make, publish, and declare this to be my last will and testament, revoking any and all previous wills and codicils by me made.

"The expense of my last illness, my funeral and the administration of my estate, wherever situated, shall be paid out of the principal of my residuary estate. . . .

"I give all my personal and household effects not otherwise effectively disposed of to my daughter, Margo Franklin, if she survives me for thirty days, or if she does not so survive me, to my executor for disbursement as he determines. . . ."

Finally, Chakaris got to the guts of the document. "I give all my residuary estate, being all real and personal property, wherever situated, in which I may have any interest at the time of my death, not otherwise effectively disposed of, to my daughter, Margo Franklin, if she survives me for thirty days. . . ."

Chakaris read on and on, finally asking if there were any questions.

"Yes," Margo said, raising her hand as if in class. "Just what did my mother leave me? What did she own that is covered by that all-inclusive paragraph?"

Chapter Five

"I'm glad you asked," Chakaris said, grinning broadly and looking at his watch. I thought of his monumental meeting at ten. "Your mother and father purchased the lovely home you grew up in back in the late fifties for eighty thousand dollars. That was an extremely high price in those days, and the home has increased in value nearly ten times.

"As you know, your mother had great and expensive taste in furnishings, all of which are included in the home. The cars were disposed of at the time of her incarceration, but virtually everything on the property and in the house and garage now belong to you.

"To the best of our ability in the time we had before this reading, in conjunction with professional appraisers, our firm has determined that even after inheritance taxes—if you allow us to set up the legal shelters you are entitled to and we earnestly recommend—your personal net worth will increase by just less than one million dollars."

Margo was stunned. The import of it had not sunk in. I would have asked when and where and how the acquisition would take place, but Margo doesn't think that way.

Chakaris sat grinning at her. Hilary filled her attaché, preparing to leave. Suddenly Margo spoke. "Why has my dad been making the payments on the house all these years if it's my mother's house?"

Hilary froze. The smile died on Chakaris' face. The court reporter looked puzzled but entered the question.

"Strike that," Chakaris said quickly.

"I can't," the reporter said. "I mean, I shouldn't. You know that."

Chakaris started to insist, but Hilary cut him off. "He's right, Mr. Chakaris. Let's clear this up on the record. May I?"

Chakaris nodded. Hilary began, "Are you sure, Margo?"

"No doubt. I've known it for so long that there's no question in my mind. I can remember my mother talking about how much more money we had because Daddy was making the house payment, and sometimes she'd even make fun of him for it. Once she said, 'I may not be his any more, but he's sure mine.'"

Chakaris winced. Hilary pulled her papers out again.

"Mr. Chakaris," she said, "I have a copy here of the divorce decree. It was the last document on the case and shows clearly that Mrs. Franklin won the house and all equity on it to that point, and it stipulates also that she assumes the mortgage and all subsequent responsibilities for it, including payments on the loan and interest, taxes, insurance, and any and all major or minor repairs. What do you make of it?"

"I make of it that it's all we need," Chakaris said gruffly. But it was obvious he was troubled.

"Where do we go from here?" Hilary asked.

"Get Franklin on the phone. I want to know if he made the payments after she was awarded the house, and why. Meanwhile, this session is recessed until the principals are notified."

Chakaris thanked the court reporter and told him Miss Brice would be taking over the case. Then he turned to Margo. "Don't worry, honey," he said. "I'm sure it's just a minor detail. The house was your mother's free and clear. I don't know why a man would volunteer to continue to make house payments on a house he lost in court, but regardless, that gives him no rights to it, and now it is yours. If he's really a fool, maybe he'll still make the payments on it. There are a few years' worth to go."

"He's not a fool," Margo insisted.

"I'm sorry," Amos said. "I've met him and I know better than to say he's a fool. I do want to clear this up. You realize now that we are representing your mother's estate, and thus you in this matter?"

"Yes."

"Good. Stay close to Hilary. She's a good one." And with that, he was gone much more quickly and lightly than a man his size and age should have been. He slipped into another office down the hall at about a minute before ten, and Hollis Fenton followed him, trailed by two other nattily dressed gentlemen, no doubt Henley and Whitehead.

Just before we were about to leave the mansion, Hilary caught up with us.

"Is Mr. Chakaris in his meeting already?"

43

"Yes," I said.

"I have a message for him."

"I thought you were taking over the case."

"I am, but besides talking with Mr. Franklin's attorney, I learned that the air traffic controllers' strike is on. Mr. Chakaris won't be able to go to Florida tomorrow after all."

"What did you learn from Daddy's attorney?" Margo asked.

"Let's talk about that tomorrow," Hilary said.

"No, let's talk about it now."

"I really can't. I have to give this message to Mr. Chakaris and then be available if he needs anything. I'm sorry."

"Can we wait?" Margo asked, almost desperate. I scowled at her as if it wasn't such a good idea. She ignored me. Hilary hesitated. "We'll wait," Margo decided, and she sat down.

Hilary started upstairs but turned back. Margo looked expectantly at her. "It's all right with me if it's all right with you," Hilary said finally. I shrugged. Margo nodded. "This meeting could be a long one, and Mr. Chakaris thinks there will be, uh, that it will be, um, that there might be—"

"Fireworks," Margo said.

"Right." And Hilary trotted upstairs.

"Beautiful, isn't she?" Margo said.

"For sure," I said, a little too enthusiastically.

Margo and I talked quietly on a love seat at the bottom of the stairs while a half dozen young lawyers found reasons to jog up and down the stairs on real or imagined missions to second floor offices and files. They heard little more than we did for the first half hour or so. Things seemed to be progressing so smoothly that no voices were raised.

"I'm still mad at God," Margo allowed.

"Do you want to talk about it?"

"I'm not sure. It's hard to talk about without becoming emotional."

"Then maybe this is the place to talk about it. There are enough people around so you can't become too emotional."

"Philip, I just flat don't see how God could let Mother die before I had gotten a chance to really confront her with His claims on her life. How do you answer that? How do you fit that into the formula of everything working together for good to those who love God? I love God, and the desire of my heart was that my mother receive Christ. God disappointed me; He failed me. I feel horrible saying that. I know how it sounds. But what else can I think?"

"I don't know."

"Oh, great. That's beautiful. You know, Philip, I hinted at my feelings the other day hoping to give you time to get your answer together, to marshal your theological forces. I even told you that I didn't want your platitudes because I thought that would force you to really dig for an original answer for me. I need something now, and as honest as you're being—I really appreciate your admitting that you don't know—it doesn't help me. You're failing me too."

"You're not a very nice person sometimes, Margo.

Did you know that?" She looked at me incredulously, as if wondering how I could say something so cruel at a time like this. Frankly, I wondered too, but I stayed with it. "No one can please you. You want your life wrapped up in tidy little packages, labeled and ready to be opened. Answers for every problem and question. Now that you're a Christian, God owes you a smooth ride, or at least the reason for any bumps in the road."

Margo was dumbstruck. She shook her head slowly. "You have no answers, so you attack me. Is that it?"

"To you, not having all the answers *is* an attack. An attack of realism. Who ever told you that life with God would be rosy? You want to be biblical? Look at Job. What did he do to deserve what he suffered? He was tormented *because* he was godly. Satan attacked him for that very reason. He was a pawn in a spiritual chess game. Is that fair?"

"You're evading my question. How does God explain promising me the desires of my heart and that everything works together for good to those who love Him, and then allowing Mother to die?"

"I don't know."

"What *do* you know, Philip?"

"I know that you'd rather be God than Margo; and wouldn't we all? You feel you could do a better job than He does. If you had His power and might and omnipotence, you'd made it all turn out all right. You'd decide what was good and what was evil."

"Haven't you ever felt that God treated you unjustly?"

"No, I haven't, but don't you dare accuse me of some

46

false piety. My problem is self-image. I've been so convinced for so long that I'm unworthy of the love of God that I feel guilty when good things come my way and fortunate when bad things come that they weren't worse. My problem is that I feel I deserve so little from God that if He ever tried to balance the books with me, I'd lose everything."

"That *is* sick."

"Perhaps it is, Margo. At least I see it for what it is. And it at least keeps me from judging God or trying to tell Him what is right and what isn't. You know how He explained Himself to Job?"

"No, but I have a feeling you're about to tell me."

"He didn't. He merely challenged Job and asked him if he could do what God does. Could he have created all the wonders of nature? Job had to see his inadequacy. But think of Job's situation when God reminded him of all the wonders of nature. He had lost everything and was suffering."

"You're saying that God has a bigger plan and knows better than I do."

"In simple terms, yes."

"Does that mean I have to like it?"

"Would you, even if I said yes?"

"No."

"God demands only your trust and faith and confidence."

"He doesn't demand understanding?"

"He nearly forbids it. I know no one who claims to understand God. If you understand God, you are God and we don't need Him."

"The height of blasphemy."

"You got it. And have you every wondered if that verse about God giving us the desires of our hearts should not be read a different way?"

"Like how?"

"I'm no theologian, and maybe I'm way off, but since it is hard to reconcile God promising us the desires of our hearts and then allowing loved ones to die when their salvation *is* the desire of our heart, try reading the verse another way. Instead of assuming it means that God will fulfill the desires we have in our hearts, could it mean that He will dictate to us what those desires should be? In other words, God will literally give us the desires of our hearts; He will instill them in us so they will be proper and in accordance with His will."

Margo was silent for several minutes. "Do you think I'm terrible?" she asked finally.

"Of course not."

"You said I wasn't very nice sometimes."

"You're not. You're a know-it-all who gets irritated when she doesn't know it all."

"So you *do* think I'm terrible."

"No. I think you're learning."

"Don't kid yourself. I've got a lot of reading, studying, and praying to do before I buy this package. Though I must admit I am drawn to your logic."

"You mean all my I-don't-knows sound logical?"

"I'm drawn to your *un*logic then. All of Christianity is illogical, isn't it? From the creation, to Job, to the virgin birth, the cross, the resurrection—"

"Perhaps I was fortunate to have been raised with it. I

went through my periods of doubting, which forced me to study and claim Christ for myself, but sometimes I think there is value in being indoctrinated with truth."

"But think of the people who are indoctrinated with lies," Margo said.

"I have. It's scary."

Appearing suddenly at the bottom of the stairs were three or four of the law office staff. They craned their necks at raised voices from upstairs. Two men were speaking at once, and another—apparently the court reporter—was asking each to wait his turn so he could record it all.

When Hollis Fenton burst from the room, yanking on his knee-length overcoat, the personnel in front of us parted like the Red Sea. We stared full into Fenton's flushed face as he sped down the stairs.

Chapter Six

A few minutes later the meeting upstairs broke up. "You're still here?" Amos said.

"I want to know what Hilary found out from Daddy's attorney," Margo said.

"Yes, well, what *did* you find?" Chakaris asked Hilary as she approached from another room. "Here let's go into my office. I'm in no hurry to get home now with no reason to get up early tomorrow."

Chakaris' office was the most elaborate we had seen in the mansion. His bookshelves were empty, and stuffed boxes were piled near the door, but it was not difficult to imagine how impressive it looked lined with law books and paintings. "Henley will like this office," Chakaris told Hilary, chuckling.

Hilary looked pleasantly surprised. "Mr. Henley?" she said. "Not Mr. Fenton?"

"Let's talk about it later. What's the word on Mr. Franklin?"

"Not good. His lawyer says he's been making the payments on the house since the beginning. Says he had an agreement with Mrs. Franklin that this would give him the first option on the house if she should ever list it for sale."

"No problem."

"And—"

"And?"

"And that the house would revert to him if she preceded him in death."

Margo hid her head in her hands. Chakaris leaned his massive body back in his chair, scowling. Hilary sat with her brows raised. "I know what you're wondering," she said. "You're wondering if he has it in writing. He does. Or at least his lawyer says he does. He won't part with the original though. Says he'll send a photocopy."

Chakaris told the young lawyer that a photocopy would not be any good if she wanted to check it for authenticity.

"You want *me* to check this thing out?" Hilary asked.

"It's your case, kid. You know that. I've been officially off it since the reading of the will."

"Wait a minute," Margo said, as if they were missing some basic reason that the whole conversation was pointless. "Are you telling me that you're doubting my father's word? That I'm supposed to fight him for my mother's estate? I'd never do it. Forget it. If it's his, it's his. If he wants it, I don't want it."

"Girl, you're talking about a million dollars here," Chakaris said. "I appreciate your altruism, but let's get serious. Even a peach like your father can sour when the big money comes into the picture."

"Well, I won't let him sour; he won't have to. If she put in writing that the house is his upon her death, then the house is his. No way I'll fight him for it."

"Margo," I said. "Don't you think you'd better sleep on this?"

"No amount of sleep is going to make it all right to battle over my mother's will. This is like a bad movie, and I don't want any part in it. Daddy wouldn't try to take anything that was rightfully mine."

"You're probably right about that," Hilary said. "His lawyer seemed genuinely surprised that your mother had left you the house."

"I was surprised too," Margo said. "Perhaps she just forgot about the deal with Daddy."

"Your mother never forgot a detail in her life," Chakaris said. "Something really stinks here, and I'm going to find out what it is. I don't mind telling you that part of my reason is financial. If the house was included in the estate illegally, it considerably lessens the base value of the estate, from which we determine our percentage as executors."

"Amos, I'm disappointed," Margo said.

"Don't be. It's strictly business, and I'm trying to make you see that people will be hurt in this, whether you care about yourself or not. I'll no longer be with the firm anyway, so it won't affect me. Are you aware that I represented your mother gratis in her trial? Her funds were depleted quickly, and we're talking about tens of thousands of dollars' worth of legal fees."

"Why did you offer that?"

"I didn't. I tried to tell her not to worry about it for the time being, but she felt terrible about it. Your father tried to pay me, but I refused that, too. Your mother finally told me that she wanted our firm to try to sell her house if

53

her appeal failed, and that we could take our fees from the profits, which would have been considerable after all these years of building equity."

"And she never told you Daddy was making the payments?"

"Never."

Margo was nearly in tears. "I don't understand any of this. Why would Daddy pay for the house unless he was going to get it someday? And why would Mother leave it to me if she knew it was illegal? She had to know it would never happen and would only cause me embarrassment."

Chakaris tried to be gentle. "Margo, it wasn't beyond your mother to do numbers on people. The last will was dated several years after your parents' divorce. She was willfully writing your father out of her will. That was the whole point of redoing it. We need to respect that."

"Was the will written after she had been arrested? I mean, if not, why hadn't she written me out when I was trying to expose her?"

Chakaris fidgeted. "She tried to. She wanted me to tear up her will and make you and your father fight over the estate. I told her your father would have no claim on it as a divorcee and that *you* would lose most of it to the state if she had no will. She still wanted to do that, but she never got around to it."

"This really brings back bad, bad feelings," Margo admitted. "I can't stand the thought of inheriting any part of that house or property now."

"Don't speak too soon," Chakaris said. "I'd never forgive myself if I let you sneeze at a million dollars.

Anyway, you don't think your mother still felt that way at the end, do you?"

"I don't know."

"Yes, you do, Margo," I said. "You know she was very fond of you and showed it in her own feisty ways."

Margo nodded miserably. "This was supposed to be the end of my mother in my life," she said. "I knew it would be tough, but I thought it would be over after tonight. Pick up a few pieces of furniture and some keepsakes and be done with it. Now this."

"It's late," Hilary said. "Why don't you get some sleep, and we'll talk strategy tomorrow."

"There will be no strategy," Margo said. "But sleep does sound good." She looked at me. "Home, James," she said, still wry to the end.

Chakaris caught my arm on the way out. "Whatever you do," he said, "don't let her talk to her father. Anything she says to him or to his representative at this point could jeopardize her rights to the estate."

"Are you confident of her rights?"

"Until I see that document Mr. Franklin's lawyer claims to have. If it's legit and dated after the will I read tonight, we've got problems."

"What time is it in Los Angeles?" Margo asked in the car.

"About ten, I guess."

"I want to call Daddy from Earl's office before I go to my apartment."

"I can't let you do that."

"What are you talking about, Philip? You don't own

me. You can't tell me what to do." I knew she didn't intend to sound so mean, but neither had I intended to sound so possessive.

"It's just not a good idea, Mar. You're dead tired. It's been a big, emotional day. Your father is gun-shy of you right now anyway because he knows he should have come to the funeral. Don't put him on the spot now."

"All I want to know is whether he wants the house, knowing that Mother left it to me in her will. If he does, then I won't fight him for it."

"That's just what Chakaris doesn't want you to say to your dad or to anyone representing him."

"Chakaris is representing me, not me him, you know."

"Correction. Hilary is representing you. And she's worth listening to."

"And worth looking at, judging by your reaction."

"Guilty."

"I can hardly believe my father has representation already. He doesn't need a lawyer to fight with me. I'm easy." Margo fell silent, thinking. "Do you really not want me to call Daddy tonight?" she asked suddenly. "Or are you just parroting Amos?"

"Both."

"I'll wait," she said.

The lights were on in Haymeyer's office when we pulled in. Earl and Bonnie were still at work. After we greeted them, I insisted that Margo go to bed, and I stayed to talk to Earl.

"Chakaris called about a half hour ago and told me the whole story," Earl said. "It's hard to figure. Mr.

Franklin always hit me as such a Milquetoast. This isn't his style."

"What do you think Amos is going to do?"

"I know what Amos is going to do. He's hired the best detective agency in the Chicago area to investigate the thing and report back to one Heather Bruce or Hilary Brewster or—" Haymeyer dug through his notes.

"Hilary Brice," I said.

"Right. And the aforementioned detective agency is assigning its top—and only—junior staff member to the case."

"You're kidding. You don't think that's a conflict of interest?"

"Just because you're in love with one of the principals? Hardly. Anyway, I don't have time for a drive to California."

"Drive? You want me to drive?"

"You wouldn't want Hilary Bruce, or Brice, to drive out there all by herself any more than Amos does, would you?"

"Well, no, but drive?"

"That air traffic controllers' strike is indefinite, in case you hadn't heard. They're not even scheduled to talk for ten days. Nationwide commerce is going to be crippled."

"And the road full of trucks."

"You'll be driving one yourself."

"I can't drive a truck."

"Not a truck really. A four-wheel-drive job."

"Margo's going to want to go, you know."

Haymeyer frowned. "What do you think, Bonnie? Should I let Margo go?"

"You won't be able to keep her home," the secretary said.

Chapter Seven

"We've got the expense of two hotel rooms all along the way anyway," Haymeyer explained the next morning. "Margo, you can stay with Hilary."

Haymeyer said he would have Bonnie or the secretary in the Chakaris law firm arrange a meeting time with Mr. Franklin and his lawyer to officially examine the documents on both sides. Chakaris thought it would put the pressure on Mr. Franklin if Hilary went immediately and offered to let him see the will and all the attendant papers. "He can either put up or shut up," Chakaris summarized, according to Earl.

Bonnie helped map out our route, arranging for the rented four-wheel drive to be delivered, making hotel reservations, and checking the weather. "It should be clear sailing except maybe in the mountains," she said. "You seldom hear of much trouble in mid-April."

Margo and I busied ourselves packing as lightly as we could. She was anxious to see her father and wanted to call him and let him know she would be there, but Haymeyer and Hilary thought the surprise would be better. "Plus, anything you say now could threaten our part of the negotiations."

Margo insisted that she didn't care and vowed she would turn the house over to her father if he wanted it, whether he was legally entitled to it or not. "If he wants it that badly, I want him to have it. He must want it for some reason or he would never push it this far. He's never hurt a flea; he surely wouldn't hurt me on purpose."

Once, such talk spilled over in front of Haymeyer, and Margo started in again on the idea that God seemed distant and hard to understand. I was able to shut it off without being too obvious and tried to scold her later. "You don't want to throw a barrier in Earl's way, do you?" I said. "When the time comes to really challenge Earl to consider God in his life, we don't want to have posed unnecessary questions for him."

"You want me to be dishonest?" Margo said. "I do have questions about God and why He did this—I mean why He allowed this. I guess I agree that we have no right to challenge God's right to do what He wants, but what happens when we don't like what He does?"

"Then we tell Him He's wrong and that we could do better. We become proud and we become God and run the universe the way we want."

"If only I could," Margo said.

"You don't mean that."

"The point is that I can't. I have no power next to God. He does what He wants. People die and people hurt and people starve and things go wrong, and we are powerless to do anything about it. He lets it happen for His own reasons, and we just have to accept it."

"Can't argue with that," I said.

"But we don't have to like it."

"Of course not."

"You were close to convincing me with your Job argument, Philip, and while I confess I haven't read it yet, I assume I shouldn't argue with it if it's God's own example of answering my questions for someone else. It's His prerogative to ignore the question and change the subject to get His point across. But why is He piling one thing on top of the other, just when I'm about to get whatever point He has for me?"

"What do you mean?"

"This thing with Daddy. Has he had a personality change? Is he a Mr. Hyde? This is not the man I knew. I went through this with my mother. Do I have to face it with my father too? I don't know if I can take it. Why, Philip? Why?"

"I don't know."

"You know, your honesty used to thrill me, refresh me, uplift me. Now it irritates me."

"And how would you like a platitude instead? A sermon maybe? A trumped-up truism?"

"No, thanks. I get the point. But I still don't like it. Be patient with me, will you? And just ignore me."

"Yes and no. I will be patient, as long as you realize what a tough position you put me in sometimes. But no, I will not ignore you."

"I mean ignore me when I'm mean. I don't want to hurt you. I'm lashing out at God and things I can't control and I'm hitting you. I'm sorry. And what do you mean, the tough position this is putting *you* in? You mean other than that I'm shooting at you a little? That

61

should be easier to take than what *I'm* going through right now."

"True enough. Let's compete for most-worthy-to-be-felt-sorry-for, OK? I know you'd win, but sometime just put yourself in my shoes. I am expected to defend the mind of God, which I don't understand any more than you do. I'm content to trust that He knows what He's doing, because I've believed that all my life. I admit this is easy to say when the toughest breaks are coming *your* way and not mine. I don't know how I'd feel if they were tearing up my world."

"My world isn't your world?"

"I can't win."

"Yes, you can. You've won my heart in spite of yourself."

"Marry me," I said.

"Give me a few days."

"Really?"

"Of course not. You don't want a bad Christian on your hands, do you? Just don't give up on me."

"We've already been through that."

"And you won't?"

"You know I won't."

"And it doesn't shock you, my bold talk against God?"

"I'm not saying I like it, Margo, but it sure beats being phony."

"Meanwhile you want me to be slightly phony in front of our godless friends, is that it?"

"Not really phony. Judicious maybe."

"Save my doubts and fears and challenges for the ears

of someone who loves me and cares about me and who won't throw over his faith in the face of my tirades?"

"Are you being facetious?"

"Not until I got into that. Then it sounded pretty good."

I laughed. "Then you're right. That's what I want."

"Fair enough," she said.

Bonnie arranged an ambitious schedule. "With three drivers you should be able to make North Platte, Nebraska, in twelve or thirteen hours the first day," she said. "You're confirmed in two rooms at the Holiday Inn. It has a lot of features, but you'd better ignore them, eat well, and sleep long because I have you down for Cedar City, Utah, the next night. If you make that, you should be able to make L.A. the next evening, maybe even late afternoon."

"North Platte and Cedar City?" Margo said. "Sounds like the big time."

We were scheduled to leave the following Monday morning, and a meeting was set with Mr. Franklin for late Thursday morning. I had to coax Margo to go to church with me in Winnetka Sunday morning, hoping that the sermon would be on Job or the sovereignty of God or some other divinely coincidental topic that would illuminate her mind and prove that I had been right—not for my sake, but for hers.

But the sermon was on the love of God, the very attribute Margo was doubting. She listened intently and seemed to enthusiastically join in the singing and other aspects of the worship service, but I couldn't get her to talk about it later. "This is something I'm really going to need to work through, Philip," she said.

The next morning Hilary, Margo, and I pulled out of Glencoe and headed south to Interstate 80 and then to points west. I took the first driving shift of four or five hours, then Hilary would go four and Margo three. The girls brought books and magazines and snacks, but nothing was opened as the three of us got to know each other for a few hours.

After telling everything we knew about Amos and Earl, for the benefit of whoever among us knew the least, we told every joke we knew to avoid talking about ourselves. Then we could avoid it no longer.

Hilary was as curious about us as we were about her. She had followed the story of Virginia Franklin's murder trial in the papers and had been fascinated by the bits and pieces she had heard about Margo's and my relationship.

We filled in the blanks as best we could, and Margo even explained how she had come to believe in Christ as a result of my concern for her and the many things I had given her to read. She suggested that Hilary could have any of those to peruse if she wished, but Hilary politely refused.

"I hadn't realized how religious you two were," she said, matter-of-factly, "though Amos warned me—ah— told me a little about you. Earl said something too about the fact that you go to church a lot and all that. I hope you won't spend the whole trip trying to convert me," she added with a smile.

"From what?" Margo asked, as only she could.

Chapter Eight

"From nothing," Hilary said. "My father's parents had been pretty strict Baptists, I understand, and when he couldn't live up to their standards, there was a falling out that never fully healed. Religion is simply not discussed when his parents are around, and they never visited on Sundays because they couldn't stand to see him drinking beer in front of the TV when they thought he should be taking his family to church."

"So you didn't go to church at all?" I asked.

"Not really. My mother had been raised to go to church on holidays and sometimes sent us or let us go if other kids invited us. We went to summer Bible school and stuff like that, but I don't remember being in church just for a meeting since I was about ten."

Hilary was the third of four girls, had always been exceptionally tall and self-conscious about her looks, never dated much until college, and decided that she had been driven to succeed in school and a career by the desire to please her parents. "They weren't pushy or prestige-oriented," she said, "but take my father, for instance. All his goals are intrinsic. He has no qualitative or quantitative goals. All he wants is to be the best he can be at a given project. If it's working around the house, he doesn't have to build the best patio deck in the neighborhood or one that would fool a professional carpenter. He just wants to do the best he can do, and he doesn't worry about anything else."

"Not a bad philosophy," I said.

"My mother is the same way," Hilary continued. "She cared more about the fact that we were honest and displayed good sense than that we were popular or beautiful or anything else."

"Then how do you explain your sort of overachievement?" Margo asked. "You know what I mean."

"Sure. I guess it's just part of my dad's philosophy. I never had a goal of being a top student so I could qualify for law school. And I certainly never set out to be on the staff of the law review. I sent resumes everywhere, just like all the other graduates, but because I had done well in school and had written in the review, I guess the people at CFH and W were impressed, and I was asked to come for an interview."

"How many other students were invited?"

"Only a few. CFH and W interviews only about ten a year and hires just one."

"And you were it."

"Right. Two years ago."

"You've been there just two years and you're already a junior partner?!"

"I didn't strive for that, either."

"What did you strive for?"

"I just wanted to prove to myself that I was worthy of being hired. I spent a lot of time in the law library, and I did my homework. I worked a lot harder my first six months on the job than I did in my last year of law school."

"That's hard to believe," I said, "from what I've heard about law school."

"I'm not saying law school wasn't grueling. It was. Almost overwhelming. And I didn't exactly love it, though some students do—if you can believe them. I was intrigued by the law and wanted to do my best, and I felt my sex was a hurdle too. Right or wrong, I felt I had to be better than the men to be considered as good."

"It worked."

"I guess. Anyway, that first six months on the job in Chicago I worked as if I was afraid I would wake up and find that I had not landed a position with one of the most prestigious firms in Chicago."

"Then you did care about prestige."

"I'd lie if I said I didn't, but it wasn't most important. It was satisfying. It said to me, 'You're doing it. You're being the best you can be.' That didn't mean I had to become a junior partner within the first year and a half, and I'm serious when I say I have no bigger goals than that. I can't imagine remaining a junior partner until I'm fifty, but I would be satisfied if I did that job the best I could do it."

"Don't be silly," Margo said. "You'll be a partner before you're thirty, a judge by forty, and on the supreme court by fifty." We all laughed, but I wonder if any of us doubted that Hilary Brice could be such a pioneer if she really wanted it. The fact that she didn't

67

live and die for it might be what would make it happen one day.

"I just want to keep doing my homework," Hilary said. "I treat every case as my top priority. I give it all I've got, give it the hours it needs, count on no one else to do my digging for me, listen to every bit of advice— from the partners I respect to the partners I don't respect, and from the colleagues I admire to the ones I don't. I don't apologize for it, and I don't talk about it much— which will be hard for you two to believe after I've gone on about it so."

"No," Margo and I said in unison. "It's fascinating," I said.

"Well, it wasn't fascinating to all my colleagues when I was named a junior partner," Hilary said. "And there was a partner who wasn't thrilled either."

"Mr. Fenton?" I ventured.

"I don't hide that well, do I?" Hilary said.

"No, it *was* rather chilly in the hallway the other night."

"I really shouldn't talk about it," she said, digging out her camera. We were quiet for more than an hour before she broached the subject again. "This isn't like me," she said, "but you two have told me so much about yourselves that I feel like I want to tell you about Hollis Fenton. You must swear to never mention it to anyone, especially Earl Haymeyer. He knows too many people that Amos knows."

We were all ears. Hilary wasn't really ready to tell us much yet, however. She wanted to apologize in advance some more first. "I live alone, you know, and there aren't many people I can tell when I have a personal problem. I shouldn't make this sound like it's still a problem, because I handled it, but I always wished I had had someone I could tell about Hollis. I mentioned it to Amos once and I think that really cooked things for Mr. Fenton. At first I was afraid Amos would defend his old friend, but there had been enough other bad reports that it was merely the straw that broke the camel's back."

"Are you going to tell us this story?" Margo asked with a twinkle.

"Probably not," Hilary said. "From this you wouldn't get the idea I'd be any good in court, would you?"

"No, but you probably are."

"Well, Mr. Fenton, who had been out of town when I was hired and who has always had a problem with women lawyers, refused to be impressed, even when good reports came back about my court appearances. He resisted the other partners' efforts to have me promoted to a junior partner."

"But he couldn't garner another vote, right?" I asked, remembering Chakaris' explanation of a few nights before.

"That's right. But I discovered later that my being voted in as a junior partner really took away Hollis' bait for me."

"His bait?"

"At one point during the earliest days of my tenure at CFH and W, Mr. Fenton called me at home and invited me out to dinner with him. It was strictly an invitation to a dinner date, no way around it. I laughed and asked if he

69

were serious and if he knew I was just out of law school—the implication being that I was about forty years his junior. He said he was quite aware of it and that if it didn't bother me, it didn't bother him.

"I could hardly respond. I was in awe of this man who had such a reputation in the courtroom. I was nearly speechless in his presence, and now, on the phone, when I realized he was serious, I didn't know what to say. I told him I thought it did bother me, though I was flattered. The man has a son at a law firm in the suburbs, who is forty years old!"

"Fenton still married?"

"Divorced. Twice. And the kids from neither marriage can stand him. He is feuding with members of both families, though there is one son he tries to stay next to for some reason. Those were not exactly amicable splits. He's quite the ladies' man. He is often seen with women, usually younger than he, but not quite forty years younger."

"So what happened?"

"Well, he was dumbfounded. I got the impression he had never been turned down before, especially by a subordinate. He immediately tried to pretend he had been kidding and said, 'Seriously, Mr. Chakaris asked that I take you to dinner and counsel you about procedures at the firm.' I couldn't call him a liar, so I accepted.

"At dinner he was so complimentary it was embarrassing. He didn't try to take my arm or anything, but he treated me like a date and I kept having to get him back onto the subject of the law firm. He told me nothing that the secretary hadn't been telling me for days. I played it very icy the whole evening, and when he walked me to my apartment door I just thanked him and went in."

"Just like you did the other night, shutting the door on him?"

"I didn't do that."

"Yes, you did."

"I did? It's second nature to me anymore."

"Why? Aren't you afraid of him?"

"I was, but I decided that if I told Mr. Chakaris what happened and he told me that I should humor the man, I would simply quit. No job is worth that."

"Did you tell Amos?"

"Sure. And Fenton got in trouble, but not before he got into more trouble with me. After I told Mr. Chakaris—and it was obvious that Amos was upset with him—Hollis made a pass at me in the library at the law offices. Nothing gross, he just leaned over my shoulder at a table and whispered that being nice to him could mean good things in my future at the firm, especially since he was the heir apparent. I told him, without whispering, that the best thing for my future at the firm would be if he kindly left me alone."

"What did he do?" Margo asked.

"It stood him straight up. He flushed and said that I would regret that. I told him I doubted it."

"Would you have been so bold if you hadn't known of Chakaris' disapproval of his actions?"

"Are you serious? I don't know what I would have done if I hadn't had someone on my side. And someone who ran the firm, no less. I guess Hollis's courtroom theatrics had gradually gone from effective to ridiculous, and he was beginning to embarrass the firm occasionally. He was still a top lawyer, one of the best, but people were beginning to wonder about him, mostly people within the profession. Judges, too."

"So did he get into trouble with Chakaris?"

"You bet. He was taken off one important case, told to leave me alone—which he didn't—and was generally scolded by Chakaris, his lifelong friend and associate."

"He didn't leave you alone?"

"He told me that squealing 'like a schoolgirl' would keep me from progressing. When I became a junior partner, he was whipped. He has been civil to me only in front of strangers ever since, and then he is so sickeningly sweet that I can't take it."

"So what happened the other night in the big meeting of the partners?"

"I thought you'd never ask. Isn't it my turn to drive, by the way?"

I had driven for six hours without thinking of the time.

Chapter Nine

We were still short of Des Moines, Iowa, when we· made our first pit stop with the gauge nearly on empty. Hilary took over at the wheel, and except for being a little tentative pulling out of the service station and onto the freeway, she handled the vehicle as if she had driven one all her life.

"Would you believe Hollis Fenton began actually trying to sabotage my cases?"

"No, I wouldn't," I said. "I can see all the rest, but isn't that a little childish for a man his age?"

"Isn't all the rest of it childish for a man his age?" Margo argued. "I believe it. What did he do?"

"I would get a message in court that 'someone from your office called and told you to call in before the hearing.' I would call and there would be no message. Then there might be a message to ignore some portion of my research because 'someone at the office said they had found further information on the subject and that it would have a bearing.'

"So I'd put off a crucial argument, hoping for some new insight someone had dug up for me, only to find out that no one at the office knew what I was talking about."

"Did it cost you any cases?"

"No, but very nearly. A couple of times I really had to scramble to salvage something for my clients."

"How did you know it was Fenton?"

"Legally speaking, I never did. It was just a gut feeling. Who else would it have been?"

"I don't know," I said. "Got any other enemies?"

"Not that I know of. I suppose there could be any number of jealous people of both sexes in my life, but I certainly have never done anything to cause it, at least willfully."

"I believe you," Margo said, "as much as I hate to be sympathetic to beautiful women. I do believe you."

I noticed a lot of snow piled on the shoulders of the interstate, though the road itself was dry and fast. We were making good time, but as the snow began to look fresher and more recently plowed, I began to hope that we weren't coming into something bad. When it was Margo's turn to drive, I told her to watch for wet roads ahead. "We'll probably have sunlight until we hit Grand Island or maybe even North Platte, but we could hit the tail end of whatever left these snow piles." I didn't think much more about it until we encountered rain, and then sleet, and were forced to slow to about thirty-five miles an hour.

I didn't like the looks of the huge snowflakes that were not exactly melting instantly on the interstate. The going was slow, but Margo refused to let me take over driving. And she was doing well. It was dark by the time we spotted the Holiday Inn at North Platte, and the snow caused deep slush puddles.

Bonnie had been right. The Inn was lovely, spacious, well-equipped. We had a leisurely dinner, and much too much to eat, and I told the women to be ready at six in the morning because we wanted to get to the end of this snowstorm. The truckers and other veteran cross-country travelers were already rumoring ten to twelve inches by morning. The eternal optimist, I believed it would stop and that our vehicle could get us through. When I peeked out in the morning, I wasn't so sure. I just wish I had had the sense to sit tight and keep our beautiful, comfortable rooms.

Margo was still getting ready when I went past their room, and Hilary slid their suitcases out into the hallway. I lugged them down to the car and wished I had brought more than a light jacket. The four-wheeler was buried in a drift, and I was forced to dig around for an old book to scrape the snow away. I hadn't dreamed of packing a scraper, let alone a pair of gloves. My hands were red and raw by the time I jumped in and started the engine. Still Margo and Hilary had not appeared. It wasn't like Margo to take long getting ready. In the rearview mirror I saw Hilary signaling me to come back in.

"What's up? Roads closed?"

"No, Margo just got a call from Earl. You want to talk to him?"

We skipped back up to their room, and I waited for Margo to finish. She looked troubled as she handed me the phone.

"There's an opening in a qualifying class for the detective school," Earl said. "Just wanted her to know about it. She'd have to start Wednesday morning. May not get another chance like this for ages."

"Oh, boy," I said with a sigh. "What do you think, Earl?"

"It's totally up to you guys. If she's serious about wanting to study this field, she'd better give it some thought."

"We don't have much time for thinking. We've got to get going to get out of this snowstorm, and if she's heading back, we can run her to the bus station right now."

"Let me know now," Earl said. "Bonnie can meet her at the station here."

"What's the word, Margo?" I said.

"I want to see Daddy," she said.

"She wants to go with us, Earl," I said, but Margo waved me off.

"It's going to be a painful meeting anyway," she said.

"Hold a minute, Earl."

"I'd better go back," she said. "I want to do this, and I don't want to know if Daddy is trying to do anything wrong. Tell Earl I'm coming back."

It felt strange without Margo with us. I found myself a little formal, more inhibited with Hilary than I had been the day before. "This is going to change our driving schedule," I said. "You want me to drive halfway and you take the rest?"

"Let's play it by ear," she said. "You may get tired driving that long. Maybe we should each drive until we need more gas, then switch."

"Whatever," I said.

"Yeah, whatever."

The interstate was already confined to one lane in each direction. Snow was whirling and blowing, and the gigantic flakes splattered against the windshield like cupfuls of rain. The four-wheeler handled the deep drifts all right, but after a half hour of slow going, we found ourselves last in a several-miles-long line of cars and trucks. When we hit a bend in the road, we could see how far the cars stretched out ahead of us. The radio already told the news of road closings heading east.

"That's encouraging," I said. "Maybe we're heading away from the trouble."

"Maybe."

I gripped the wheel too tightly and tired quickly.

Hilary tried to read, but the ride was too bumpy. She gave up. "You really love Margo, don't you?" she said.

"Yes, I really do."

"And you've worked through the idea that it might have been pity at first, because of her situation, I mean?"

"Yeah, we have. It *was* pity at first. But not now."

"That's nice. I don't think I've ever been in love."

"Well, I thought I was once before. I was engaged. There was no doubt in my mind that I was in love. It didn't work out and was painful for a while. But when I fell in love with Margo, it was so different, so incredible, that I knew I had never really loved before. Whatever it had been, it wasn't love. This, what I feel for her, is love."

"How do you know?"

"I just do. I love her so much that I would give her up

if I was convinced that I was not what was best for her. I think that's a good definition of love."

"Is it yours?"

"I wish it was. Actually, it took me a long time to come to that way of thinking because I loved Margo so much that I was selfish and possessive about it. In fact, that philosophy is Margo's. She said it first, and I thought I could never duplicate it, though I knew I should."

"And now you really feel that way?"

"I do."

"Margo is a very special lady. I can tell. She's a deep thinker, in spite of her self-image problem."

"That was obvious to you?"

"A little. Of course, I know she's under great strain right now. That would take the self-confidence out of anyone."

"Where'd you get yours?"

"My what? My air of self-confidence?"

"Yeah."

"I don't know. I've always had it. People have always said that until they got to know me they thought I was arrogant. My profession hasn't helped. Neither has my height."

"But you're not cocky."

"I know that, but did *you* know it when you first met me?"

"No, I guess I thought you were pretty self-assured, especially the way you treated Hollis Fenton."

"Really that bad, huh?"

"I don't know. You made it appear as if he deserved it

for some reason. And I guess he did."

"Anyway, I think most of my image is a result of shyness. I know I express myself well when I am forced to, and I enjoy speaking in meetings and in court, being in command of taking a deposition, or whatever. But unless it's all scoped out in advance and I'm prepared, I'd rather be in the background. Not easy for a woman of my height."

"Or beauty."

"Thank you."

"So you overcompensate?"

"I guess. I've never thought about it, but I know it doesn't do any good to try to act *un*arrogant or *un*conceited, if there are such words. You have to be yourself, and I just have to try to assure people that I don't think I'm anyone special, if I ever get the chance."

"I believe you, but you're wrong."

"I don't follow," she said.

"I believe that you don't think you're anyone special, just like I believe that you don't think you're beautiful. But you're wrong on both counts. Don't argue. The fact that you don't think you're anyone special is one reason you're so special. And not knowing how beautiful you are gives you a certain innocence that enhances even your beauty."

"Can we talk about something else?"

"I suppose we ought to."

But we didn't. We just didn't talk. The snow nearly belched from the sky in great waves. Visibility went to nil. More than once the great line of cars—now stretching farther than we could see in both directions—

slipped and skidded to a stop, first for five minutes, then for twenty-five. A couple of times I jogged ahead to help push someone back onto the road. More and more it appeared that we might spend several hours stopped there. I was glad we had a full tank of gas. A six-pack of Cokes and a bag of pretzels didn't sound too appetizing to either of us, but it was all we had.

We were too far from anything to walk anywhere in this weather, and the sight of CB-equipped trucks in front and behind was comforting. At least they had news. Part of the news was that from North Platte east was open. Margo would get home. From where we were back to North Platte, however, just a few miles, was closed. We could see the result of it across the median. Miles upon miles of cars were going nowhere.

And the snow continued.

Chapter Ten

We drove at ten miles an hour or so for several minutes, watching cars slide off the road on both sides. There was nothing to say. Both of us were hoping something would break so we could either get out of the storm area or find a spot to settle in and wait it out. No one wanted to be stranded in a car all day and night on a snowy highway, even with fuel and a little food.

We were city people. I was not skilled in survival. I was willing to ration the food and use the engine sparingly, but the thought of just shutting the windows against the snow and being buried under drifts scared me.

When the line of cars stopped and two semis jackknifed on a bridge ahead, I started talking again, just to get my mind on something else. There was nothing else to do; they were too far ahead for me to run and help, and there appeared to be many people helping already. I wondered if we would move again at all that day.

"So, what happened to Hollis Fenton the other night?"

Hilary finished her paragraph, bent back the corner of the page, closed the book, and tucked it under the front seat. "One lousy book," she said. "You'd have to be stranded in the snow on a trip across country with no one interesting to talk to, to keep reading that thing."

"So what's the verdict? You gonna keep reading or have you found someone interesting to talk to?"

"I'm all ears."

"No, you're not. You missed the question."

"Don't kid yourself. I'm just not sure I want to talk about him anymore."

I was disappointed, but I knew it wouldn't be right to push. "Suit yourself," I said.

"OK, I'll talk about him," she said quickly, with a smile. "I just didn't want to appear too anxious."

College-aged kids in the car in front of us jumped out in shirt-sleeves to throw snowballs at cars and trucks across the median. The eastbound traffic wasn't moving, and probably wouldn't for hours until the state police could route them to open exits, so the little battle made the drivers' day. Many leaped out of their vehicles, laughing and retaliating. Our car was pummeled, but we weren't dressed for battle, so we just sat it out.

"He was, in effect, put on probation by the other partners, according to Amos. That means he is still a partner but will be listed second to last, just ahead of Amos, on the letterhead. The firm will be called Henley, Whitehead, Fenton, and Chakaris."

"How did Hollis take it?"

"You saw as well as I did. Amos said Hollis told the partners not to be too quick to print the new stationery.

And then he rushed from the room. Amos thinks he was just blowing air. He's known Hollis a long time, through the good days and now the bad."

"Is the man incompetent?"

"I don't think so, and if anyone has a reason to think so, I do. I just think he's terribly proud and hates to have his feathers ruffled. He needs the job and the money and the prestige. Neither of his former wives have remarried, so his money is really chewed up by the time he sees much of it."

"How much would a guy like that make?"

"Oh, a few hundred thousand a year, I assume. The firm has been thriving for years, and he *is* a full partner. I don't think he has the guts to give that up. He still has the makings of a great lawyer. Sort of like an athlete who's past his prime but whose skills still put him ahead of most younger men."

"What *are* his skills?"

"Same as with any good lawyer. A good memory, a quick mind—especially on his feet or under pressure, though that's the skill that's eroding the fastest—persistent. That's the one he still has. He never gave up on me, first pursuing me and then trying to make things rough for me. He just never quits."

"Those could be wonderful characteristics in a nice guy."

"Absolutely. Also horrible in a dictator. Or a Hollis Fenton."

"So you don't think he'll quit the firm?"

"I don't, but who can tell what he might do? The demotion will be obvious and will humiliate him. I think what hurt him most was that he got no support from Amos, and they go back such a long way. Amos's official resignation became effective before the vote on the new lineup."

"Amos told us," I said. "Could it have happened the other way around?"

"Sure. It was totally Amos's decision. He could have hung in and voted before bailing out, but he would have had to vote against his old friend, so he did it this way."

"In effect he still voted, right?"

"Right. I just hope Hollis gets this thing settled in his mind, licks his wounds, and doesn't do something rash. He could join another firm, and there are plenty who would jump at the chance to get him, but he would likely try to do harm to our firm either by stealing clients or bad-mouthing us."

"It really puts you guys in the middle, doesn't it? Could you fire him, or vote him out?"

"The partners could. I don't think anyone wants that."

"Afraid of him?"

"Probably. Sad but true. Gone are the days when you fire the bad apple because it's the right thing to do. In earlier years, Amos might have done it. He'll leave it to Henley and Whitehead now. And they're super."

The trucks ahead had been straightened and were moving. It was several minutes before the movement affected us, and then the compact car in front of us slid sideways and couldn't move. Startling me, Hilary climbed down from the front seat and, with no more protection than a sweater over a blouse, bent at the knees and drove her shoulder into the left rear bumper, pushing the struggling car back into the deep ruts where it grabbed and began rolling. She hurried back to the accompaniment of appreciative honks from the cars behind us. I just looked at her and shook my head. "Trying to make me look like a lazy slob?" I said.

"You don't need my help," she said, ducking my playfully cocked backhand.

Still we barely crept along and by nearly noon we had covered less than fifty miles. Our schedule was shot. Even if the storm broke and the roads cleared within an hour, there was no way we'd make our next scheduled stop by that same night. Ominous weather reports on the radio made me want to keep pushing as long as even one lane was open. Hilary agreed. "I'm a pioneer all the way," she said. "Let's not quit moving until we have to."

We needed fuel and lunch so we took the exit at Ogallala, Nebraska. "Ever hear of this place?" I asked. She shook her head, neither of us realizing that it would be a place we would probably never forget. In trying to maneuver the overpass and pick my way through lines of trucks and cars already parked or stuck on both sides, I embedded us in a snowbank.

Hilary took the wheel and I rocked us from behind until the car was free, but not before the rear wheel covered me with slush. "I'm really sorry," Hilary said, laughing. "I don't know why it hits me funny. I really am sorry, even if I don't sound like it!"

Tentatively easing our way down a frontage road toward the huge truck stop that had drawn us like a mirage, I tried to blast past a stuck semi the way two pickups just had. They made it. We didn't. We were high centered in deep snow, and having nothing to dig with, we needed help this time. We couldn't even rock it, and neither of us could stand to be out in the weather for more than a few minutes at a time. For some reason, Hilary still thought it was hilarious. "I just figured out your name," I said.

I hung around outside the car, peering underneath and trying to look helpless, all the while keeping an eye out for a good Samaritan. A few people passed, but none stopped. Few cars were moving, though many were now lined up behind us. I shivered into the front seat.

"I hate to ask you to do this," I said.

"You want me to try to dig us out with something? I'll be happy to try—"

"No, you can't dig us out without a shovel, and if we had a shovel, I could do it. What I want you to do is what I just did."

"What'd you do? I didn't see you do anything but check out the situation."

"Trust me, Hilary. If you check out the situation, help will come. Don't make me explain it."

"And did you want me to stick a leg out into the road?"

"Don't be silly. If you don't want to do it, I'll understand."

"No, I'll do it." And it worked in no time. Hilary just got out, pulled her collar up against the wind, and surveyed our hopeless situation. A wrecker stopped behind us and a pickup in front. They nearly fought over the right to pull and push us out, finally agreeing to do both at the same time.

Soon we were again easing between closely parked trucks and trailers, ignoring the blocked entrance to the truck stop, and entering through the exit like everyone else. We waited in line for gas, then again for a meal, and decided to eat big in case we found ourselves stranded later. We didn't realize that for all practical purposes, we were already stranded.

After lunch Hilary waited in line to place a call back to Chicago while I picked through trinkets and junk in the attached "store" for some gloves.

"Only local calls, I guess," Hilary reported after ten minutes of trying to get a long distance operator. "You need an operator to dial outside this area, and both of them in this town must be busy."

"Be kind," I said, enjoying her. As I paid for the gloves and some more junk food to store in the car, I heard a woman at a switchboard reserving a room for a young trucker.

I asked her if she could arrange for two more rooms at the same place. "I'm pessimistic when I see all these truckers sitting around as if there's nowhere to go. They aren't willing to commit to a hotel room, but they aren't out on the road, either."

"The road west is closed after another twenty miles or so anyway," a trucker told me.

"That's all I needed to hear," I told Hilary. "Let's take those rooms if we can get 'em."

"He'll hold one room for an hour," the woman said, and she gave us directions to the Isle of Paradise.

"The Isle of Paradise," Hilary repeated. "I can't wait to see this."

"You'll have to park at the corner and walk about a quarter of a mile," the woman said. "His parking lot is closed, but the hotel is open."

Hilary stifled a laugh.

"You're a snob," I said.

Chapter Eleven

On the other side of the freeway, the bespectacled man behind the counter at the Isle of Paradise looked haggard. "This started yesterday, you know," he said. "A lot of the people who were stranded here last night want to keep their rooms in case they come back. They're out looking for open roads and if they're back by one, I've got to let them stay."

He looked as if he'd been there all night, and I soon learned that he had. "I can't plow the parking lot because the plow is in my garage at home. My wife can't even get from the house to the garage, so I'll be replacing the linens myself today. If everybody can just be patient, I'll get around to you."

Everyone in the lobby pledged their undying cooperation and sympathy for the owner's plight in exchange for one of the precious rooms, to be paid for in advance. And such rooms. It was obvious when we first got a look at ours that it would never work.

It was tiny, tacky, and dominated by one double bed. "It looks like I'm sleeping in the car," I said. Hilary just laughed. As a tribute to modern commercialism, the room was built around a beautiful color television that carried one local station and a cable hookup that showed Atlanta Braves baseball games, of all things. Hilary sat on the edge of the still unmade bed. I stood awkwardly watching "I Love Lucy."

"I'll check back at the office," I said. "You want to try calling Chicago again?"

A few minutes later I was back with the good news that a young man next to us—who found himself in a suite of two private rooms with two beds—was willing to trade with us. But Hilary was still on the phone, and she did not look happy. I didn't make her tell me what it was all about until we had switched rooms.

"There's no phone in here," she noticed immediately. So it would be TV, messages taken at the office downstairs, awkward conversations, and isolated sleeping rooms until the weather cleared. Hilary had seemed amused by it all until she had placed that call.

"What's up?" I asked.

"I'm not supposed to tell you, Philip, but I'm not going to be able to keep it from you."

"What?"

"Margo sent a message to Earl. It said not to worry about her and that she would be back in a week or so."

"Where's she going?"

"Didn't say."

"No clue?"

"I guess not."

"Earl worried?"

"Not really. He thinks she can take care of herself, but he's not excited about the idea that she's missing this detective school opportunity."

90

"That bothers me too, but I'm more worried about the fact that she started whatever trip she's on in a snowstorm and that she didn't communicate with me."

"She told him to tell you, but he didn't want to. He doesn't want you to worry, and he feels it's important that we get to California."

"Where would she be going?"

"That's what I was going to ask you, Philip."

I was worried. She had not been in the best frame of mind lately, but whom could she go to? I wasn't aware of any friends she had between Nebraska and Chicago. What would be important enough for her to pass up this school opening she had been so excited about?

"Philip, there's something else."

"Hm?"

"There's something else. Something I haven't even told Earl yet. Mr. Henley's secretary told me they received a photocopy of Mr. Franklin's alleged agreement with Virginia Franklin about the house."

"Does it look legitimate?"

"Yes, and it could nullify the will Amos read for Margo. It calls for Mr. Franklin to keep making payments on the house for the extent of the mortgage and to pay Margo fifty thousand dollars on Mr. Franklin's acquisition of the property. It was dated later and would take precedence, and there is one other very interesting clause that ties the thing together, at least in my mind.

"The clause calls for an immediate cash payment to Virginia Franklin of one hundred thousand dollars for the ownership of the estate upon her death."

"So for a hundred thousand to Virginia, fifty thousand to Margo, and the mortgage payments he's been making, he gets a million dollar estate."

"Exactly, as long as Mrs. Franklin preceded him in death."

"And who would have predicted that?"

"Our firm, for one."

"I'm lost."

"The photocopied document sent to our offices, covering Mr. Franklin's interest in the estate, was under our own letterhead. It was prepared by us, and sure enough, Mr. Henley's secretary was able to locate our copy in the files."

"How could that happen without Mr. Chakaris's knowledge, when he was the executor of her will? Doesn't that sound incredible?"

"The document was typed by a secretary no longer with the firm and carries a clause that it was to be kept confidential even from other principals in the law offices. Which is against our policy, by the way."

"Why would Chakaris violate the policy of his own law firm? And why wouldn't he remember preparing the document for the Franklins?"

"Because he didn't prepare it, Philip. The initials at the bottom of the document are H.F./G.M."

"G.M. is the secretary who typed it, and H.F. is your favorite lawyer, right?"

"Right."

"Is it contestable?"

"Mr. Henley doubts it. He's going to send it on ahead to Los Angeles so I can have a chance to study it before meeting with Mr. Franklin and his lawyer."

"Hilary, what do you think is Hollis Fenton's interest in this?"

"I don't know, but I'm especially worried about it, now that he's been shafted at the firm. It's bizarre that he hid the document from Mr. Chakaris, thus leaving Mr. Franklin with the burden of coming forward with it. Mr. Franklin probably thought we knew all about it until we called him about why he was still paying on the house. There would be no reason for the document to still be confidential once his former wife had died."

"You would have thought he would come forward immediately if he thought his interests were being ignored," I said.

"I'm sure he assumed we would be getting to him shortly for the reading of the new will. He did have a lawyer ready to talk to me, though."

"Maybe his new love put him up to that."

With nothing to do, nowhere to go, no one to call, and nothing to say, I felt like putting my fist through a window. I paced the room. Hilary kept wishing aloud that there was something she could say or do. "Let's not worry until we have to," she suggested.

We watched television and read for several hours, finally venturing out into the blowing and drifting snow to the only two restaurants open in town, both on the same street as the motel. One was a pizza place and the other was The Hungry Eskimo, which we decided was too ironic a name to qualify for our first meal. We had a pizza, but somehow it didn't seem right to eat so somberly in such a festive place. I was miserable.

We trudged back to the motel, where a message waited from Margo. "I wrote it down," the man told me. "I couldn't make much sense of it, and she didn't leave a number."

It read: "Got your number from Earl. Sorry you're stranded. Don't worry about me. I'll see you soon."

"She ain't gonna see you soon if she's tryin' to get here from anywhere," the man said with a smile. I thanked him.

"What do you suppose she meant by 'See you soon,' Hilary?"

"Don't make too much of it. It may have just been used the way we always use it. It may mean nothing."

"But nothing else she said means anything either. I have to have something to go on. Do you think someone is holding her or has intercepted her or something? Someone who wants to make sure she doesn't survive her mother by thirty days?"

"Philip, you're really reaching now. She said not to worry. Sure, someone could have forced her to say that, but you're in no position to worry about it, let alone do anything about it. You'd better take it at face value and assume she's OK. It'll drive you nuts otherwise."

It was after dark now, and as I peered out the window of our suite I had to guess we'd be there another full day and night. The snowplows cleared one lane for both directions of traffic in the town, but no one was going more than a few blocks. The interstate was closed for fifty miles in both directions, and the police weren't even letting people try the overpass to the truck stop.

"So, it's pizza or The Hungry Eskimo for as long as we're here," I said, trying to sound light.

It didn't work. Regardless of what I said on what subject, my fear and worry came through.

Chapter Twelve

By the next morning, Hilary was completely packed, her vote for total optimism, assuming we would be on the road again within a few hours. I was slouched in a chair, feet propped up on the at-least-ten-dollar "stylized" table, gloomily watching the national news out of Atlanta forevermore.

The weatherman didn't even know how to pronounce Ogallala, but he worked out a reasonable facsimile and reported that our adopted little snowbunny trap had been awarded the national Golden Shovel Award for the most snow in the shortest time—thirty inches in the past twenty-four hours.

Hilary even had her coat draped over a chair, as if ready to pop it on as soon as some all-clear signal were given. It was still snowing, albeit lightly now. I padded out to the balcony in my stocking feet and peered over the railing to the street. People were digging out cars and a few graders were clearing a little more of the main drag, but no one was really going anywhere.

"I'm going down to the office and see if anything's open," Hilary said. "Let me have the keys. I may drive to the overpass to see if we can get to the truckstop on the other side. Want anything in case I get over there?"

I said no. I had hung a six-pack of Cokes on the outside doorknob overnight, and an icy one with some cheesy tortilla chips made a sickening breakfast. It did, however, leave me less hungry. I searched the room for anything readable, but except for a local newspaper and its three-day-old prediction of spring weather, the only thing available was a Bible, "placed here by the Gideons."

I didn't even pick it up, but it prompted me to flip off the television and sit thinking and praying. My energy had been invested in worry and frustration, which even people without God would classify as a waste of time. People who claimed to live for God or who have Him living in them should have less reason than anyone for wasting time worrying. I prayed for Margo. I didn't feel much better, but I knew there was nothing else I could do.

I tried to go back in my mind to what I had been thinking before all the trouble started. It was about Earl and how afraid I was that something Margo or I would say or do would adversely affect our spiritual impression on him. I realized that it had really mattered to me because Earl really mattered to me.

Here was a guy who was more of a Christian in life-style and honesty and treatment of others than many professing Christians I had known. And yet he resisted any personal talk about Christ or the need for God in his life. I wanted to reach him, not for any selfish reason, but because he was Earl. He was the kind of a guy who would flourish in a relationship with Christ (and who wouldn't?), and about whom I cared very much.

I would never forgive myself if I spent a lot of time with Earl—especially while working for him—and never got to the point where I was able to articulate my faith to him. He knew where I stood, but he was convinced that "religion is all right for those who want it or need it."

And he didn't want it. Didn't see the need for it. Maybe his life-style was the very thing that kept him from what he really needed. And, being a lawyer, maybe Hilary could coach me on how to express myself better. While I was asking her how I could be more eloquent, maybe she would catch on to just what it was I wanted to communicate to Earl and appropriate it to herself.

I felt a little better. I had a project, something to think, talk, and pray about. It didn't lessen my worry over Margo, but at least it would assume some of the time burden in my troubled mind. I heard Hilary trotting up the stairs. It was nearly noon. The snow had stopped, but it was cold and the drifts were deep and foreboding.

"Let's get rolling, Sad Sack," she said as she knocked and entered in the same motion. I whirled around.

"You're kidding. The overpass is open?"

"I don't know about the overpass, but people are getting onto I-Eighty heading west. It's closed north where the north-south split comes at Big Springs, but we're going south through Denver at that point anyway, aren't we?"

"Yeah," I said, scrambling to throw my things together.

Soon we were part of the only traffic jam Ogallala, Nebraska, has probably ever had. There was still just one lane to be shared by cars going both directions on the main street. Local people were heading in, interstate travelers were heading out, and volunteers were holding one line of cars so the other could get through, then switching and stopping the movers so the waiters could go.

When we finally reached the stoplight three blocks from the motel, we headed left and got in line to convince the policeman on the overpass that we could make it. He wanted to know which direction we were heading. "Whichever is open," I said, wanting to get somewhere even if it meant backtracking.

"West is open for maybe twenty miles," he said. "Then you can go only south at the Big Springs split."

"Perfect. We're trying to go through Denver."

"I doubt you'll make Denver," he said. "But good luck."

It was eerie to see no cars on the other side of the median. The eastbound lanes had been closed for so long that other than a few stalled cars and trucks here and there, nothing was moving on that side. As for us westbounders, we were in a line that stretched as far as we could see, front and back, all going about twenty miles an hour and wondering why the fast-clearing sky didn't start melting the snow.

The pavement was wet but clear of snow in the one lane open to the west, but the drifts in the left lane were up to four feet deep. Though we were mobile and could have passed, there was nowhere to go. Every once in a while an eager beaver behind us would swing out into the left lane when it wasn't so deep for a stretch and try to pass a slew of cars before the big drifts rose up again. But when the driver looked for an opening to merge back in, those who had seen his folly determined to make him wait.

"You want me to drive?" Hilary said.

"No, thanks. I feel better doing something."

"So would I, but I suppose I have a little less on my mind than you do."

By mid-afternoon we had not progressed far. "If it clears soon and two lanes open, we ought to try to get as far as we can," I suggested.

"I think we ought to just hope to make Denver," Hilary said. "You're exhausted already, and this kind of driving—even for a fresh driver—is going to get old fast."

Occasionally the traffic stopped for five minutes, but the trouble—whatever it was—was so far ahead that we couldn't determine the cause. After one long stop, we passed the trouble about ten miles ahead. Two tractor-trailers had tried to open a closed exit. They got about a hundred feet into it and found themselves pushing a wall of snow that didn't want to be pushed.

At one point the whole line of westbound traffic was routed off the interstate, down an exit, through a small town and back on via a frontage road. As we exited we watched huge earthmovers attack the mountains of snow on the overpass. It was hard to believe when two lanes opened an hour and a half later and the braver souls— like ourselves—broke free and hit the speed limit. Soon we forked southwesterly toward Denver. The roads and the skies were clear and dry. The higher we got from sea level, however, the more our engine sucked air.

After one stop, where we switched places, I tried reading Hilary's book for a few minutes and gave up in disgust. "What is this, anyway?"

"Supposed to be a novel," she said. "But I think it's more of an experiment."

"Writing itself is an experiment for this writer," I said, stuffing the book beneath the seat. "Do you suppose we should have tried to contact our offices back there?"

"No. Let's call when we get to Denver. There can't be any news we can act upon unless it's 'Come home now,' and I want to see Denver anyway. I've never been there."

"Me either," I said, but I still wished we had tried to put a call through to Earl or to Hilary's office. "You gonna be hungry before this evening?"

"I don't think so," she said. "Let's just push on through. If it's this dry all the way, it shouldn't take long."

Suddenly I was exhausted. The driving had gotten to me, I guess. I also realized that I had not slept well the night before. Still worried, I was not as anxious now over Margo since directing my concern to praying for her. It had made me feel a little more positive, and I tried to take her message literally. She didn't want me to worry, and she said she would see me soon. I leaned my head against the icy window and tucked one leg underneath me. I was asleep in minutes.

When I awoke a few hours later, Hilary was picking

through a snowy mountain pass, alternately accelerating and braking, watching the rearview mirror nervously as more impatient drivers—or locals who knew the roads and conditions—flew past. "Need some relief?" I said, startling her.

"No." She looked determined. "I want this experience. Unless you're afraid for your life."

"I trust you," I said. She smiled but never diverted her eyes from the road.

"I've been wanting to talk to you," I said. "We haven't really talked all day."

"There's nothing wrong with that," she said. "We don't *have* to talk all the time, do we?"

"No, but there's something specific I want to talk to you about."

"And you're going to bring it up now, when I need every reserve ounce of consciousness to keep us alive. It's getting dark, Philip."

"I thought you lawyers had minds like steel traps, or something like that."

"It's not our minds as much as our personalities, and mine is about to tell you to keep quiet."

"Oh, I'd like to hear *that*."

"Keep quiet."

"Impressive."

It was all she could do to keep from laughing, but I knew she was right. This was no time for serious discussion, especially if we wanted to make Denver by the same night. We had no reservations, and we wouldn't be staying long because we wanted to start at about six

103

the next morning and see if we could get as far as Las Vegas.

It was Wednesday evening. By now, Hilary's office had put on hold Mr. Franklin and his Thursday morning appointment. Without further trouble, we would make Las Vegas Thursday night and L.A. Friday afternoon. "You probably should have your office set the meeting with Mr. Franklin for either late Friday night or Saturday morning," I said.

Hilary seemed distracted. "What?"

"The meeting with Franklin," I repeated. "You're going to want time to wind down before seeing him, aren't you?"

"I can't even think about that now. Tell me later the time you think we're going to arrive, and we'll go from there, OK?"

"Sure."

"Was that the big subject you wanted to discuss?" she said.

"Hardly."

"The last time we talked at much length, you were trying to convince me how beautiful I was."

"And you're even more so when you're concentrating. You should see your profile."

"Seeing my own profile is something that will never happen, Philip. I don't even have to concentrate to know that."

A sign read: "Denver—14 miles."

Chapter Thirteen

"Now I don't feel much like talking," I said an hour later after we had checked into our separate rooms and met for dinner at the hotel restaurant. "Can I save it until tomorrow on the road?"

"Please do. Did you reach Earl?"

"No, got Bonnie, though. No messages from Margo. I told Bonnie where we are and where we expect to be during the next few days. She's arranged our reservations in Las Vegas. I'll bet we'll be the only people there just to sleep before heading to Los Angeles. Did you reach your office?"

"Yes. I asked them to arrange my meeting with Mr. Franklin for Saturday morning. That will give me time to study the document before seeing him."

We had ordered and were waiting to be served. Hilary let her shoulders sag, the first time I had seen her relax her regal posture. She breathed a heavy sigh. "I'm tired," she said. "Really, really tired."

"Me too. I'm going straight to bed after dinner. You?"

"Yeah. Might call the office one more time, though. I think they should tell Earl about the document and the

105

ramifications. He shouldn't have a man on this case and not know everything."

"They haven't told him yet?"

"They were probably assuming you would, Philip. I'll tell them."

"No! What would Earl think, getting that information from someone other than me? I had no idea he didn't know yet. I just assumed—"

"You can't assume anything. You know that."

"I've got to call him right now."

A few minutes later I returned to a waiting dinner. "I got the answering machine," I said. "I can't tell him that way. I'll call him from Vegas tomorrow night."

We ran into more mountain snow and slush in Utah the next day, slowing us more than we anticipated. But it did give us lots of time to talk. "I have a problem I think you can help me with," I began. "I have always had trouble expressing myself verbally. I can write things OK, but I'm not as good when speaking."

"You mean you're better on paper than orally, not verbally."

"What?"

"Verbally. You said you had trouble verbally. Not true if you can write. That's verbal, too."

"Picky, picky."

"Well, in a sense you merely illustrated your point. Perhaps word choice is a problem."

"Perhaps, professor. May I continue?"

"I'm sorry."

"Don't be. Anyway, Hilary, here goes: You know, I

presume, that Margo and I are Christians."

"Christians? I thought you were Baptists or funda-mentalists or born-againers or something. Most people are Christians, aren't they?"

"Well, no, not really."

"Well, Philip, certainly in America, if a person isn't an atheist or an agnostic, he would be either Jewish or Christian, wouldn't he? I mean if he has any normal church background at all it is going to be Lutheran or Methodist or Presbyterian or Baptist, right?"

"See my problem, Hilary? I need to tell you why you're wrong, but it's complicated. Let me try it this way: You know certain brand names have been diluted by imitation, like Band-Aids, Kleenex, and Jeep?"

"You mean where it originated as a brand name and then became so associated with the product that people call any bandage a Band-Aid and any tissue a Kleenex?"

"Exactly. That's what happened to the term 'Chris-tian.' Originally it meant a Christ one or one like Christ. It was the term given to His early followers, who organized after His death and resurrection. They are the forerunners of the current Christian religion. But not everyone who calls himself a Christian is really a follower of Christ, wouldn't you agree?"

"Well, some may not be as devout as others, I suppose, or worry about it so much. But you're not saying that Lutherans or Presbyterians aren't really Christians just because they aren't as fundamental or old-fashioned as, say, Baptists or some others, are you?"

"What I'm saying is that not only are some Lutherans and Presbyterians not really Christians in the biblical

107

sense of the word, but neither are some Baptists or some of any other denomination you want to name. The point is not in being religious or belonging to a denomination or even going to church every Sunday. We believe a true Christian is one who believes that Jesus Christ is the only way to God and who responds accordingly by trusting in Him for their salvation."

Hilary pursed her lips and raised her eyebrows. After breathing a vapor on her window and wiping it off, she said, "OK, I see your point. You think you and Margo and those like you are the true church, sort of the way the Jehovah's Witnesses and the Mormons and even the Moonies believe they are the true church."

"Oh, boy."

"That's not it?"

How was I supposed to explain it? I stalled, studying the dashboard before answering.

"Not really. It isn't a matter of being exclusive unto ourselves. It's just that Christ Himself said He was the way, the truth, and the life and that no man could come to God except through Him."

"Then there's nothing wrong with Christianity being exclusivist, if that's what the founder, or the namesake anyway, said."

"Right. But where we differ from those other groups you mentioned is that while they call themselves Christian too, they're just as wrong as the normal, everyday churchgoer if they add something or take away something from the gospel. I mean, some of those groups really have some strange beliefs."

"And you don't?"

"Not really. Fantastic things, yes, but nothing that's not in the Bible. We believe that Jesus was born of a virgin, lived a sinless life, died in our place for our sins, and was raised from the dead."

Hilary smiled. "You've got to admit that's pretty far-fetched, but at least it's the commonly accepted belief about Christianity, from Catholicism to Protestantism. It's good to know you and Margo aren't weirdos, even if you do have some strange taboos."

"Like what?"

"Well, you don't drink or smoke or anything like that, do you?"

"No, but you don't either."

"But not because of any religious list of rules."

"Neither do we. There are Christians who are really outspoken against some things, but again, unless it's specifically in the Bible, it's simply a matter of personal conviction, not religious injunction."

"So why are you telling me all this, Philip? You in effect promised not to try to convert me on this trip."

"I don't remember that promise, but here's the reason. Margo and I believe in Christ so deeply and are so convinced that people who don't know Him are missing out on what life is really all about that we want to share Him with people. That's part of what Christianity is about. Christ told His early followers to tell the whole world about Him. We want to start with the people closest to us."

"Does that mean I should keep my distance or risk the strong-arm?"

"Forget that, will you? We don't want to tell people

who know what we mean and still don't want to hear it. Anyway, if you believed something this deeply and felt it would make a life or death difference to your friends, I would be insulted if you didn't tell me."

Hilary thought for a moment. "You're right," she said. "I suppose I'd be a little hurt if you never told me about the most important thing in your life. I would also be insulted if you did tell me when I wasn't interested in listening. Which I don't think I am. Something about it bothers me. It's an intrusion, a condescension of some kind, I think. Do you mind?"

"I hadn't really intended to tell you anything about it yet," I said. "I was really looking for advice."

"That's the story of my life, Philip. It'll cost you a hundred dollars an hour, but fire away. How can I counsel you?"

"It's Earl. We want to communicate our faith in Christ to him. We're looking for the right opening because we don't want to put him off, insult him, hurt him."

Hilary shifted in her seat in what appeared to be a vain attempt at getting comfortable. "What makes you think he needs what you've got?"

"If I explained the whole setup to you, you'd understand that we believe that everyone needs Christ. That's the point. People who know Christ and trust Him with their lives are people who have life abundant. Those who don't will never truly be happy or fulfilled."

"And they'll go to hell when they die?"

"We believe that, yes."

"Well, let me tell you something, Philip: That's not good enough. Any first year marketing student can tell you that to reach somebody with a message, you have to know what his realized needs are. I'll bet that Earl Haymeyer isn't any more worried about hell than I am. If you want to reach him on that score, you have to convince him there is a hell, and that the God you believe in would send him there unless he became a Christian. Then show him how he can escape it. Want to take bets on the outcome of that?"

"That—or something close to it—used to work, believe it or not. Still does in some cases."

"And you could make a case for the fact that just because belief in hell went out with the Dark Ages doesn't mean that it doesn't exist. I don't think it does, but regardless, it's probably the wrong tack for Earl Haymeyer."

"We haven't said anything to Earl about hell. *You* brought that up." I shot a hard glance at her.

"So you think it may be a latent fear of mine?"

"I didn't say that."

"I know. *I* did. That was the one thing I remember from my brief religious—uh—Christian exposure as a child. Really a scary deal, choosing between heaven and hell."

"Agreed. But take Margo, for instance. She didn't come to Christ out of fear of hell. Her need was to have someone forgive her and love her and give her the abundant life I mentioned before. That's what the Bible calls it."

"It does, huh? That's nice. Abundant life. But anyway, even though you feel that it's your duty to tell everyone they need Christianity—"

"That's not what we tell them, for the reasons we talked about. The wrong evolvement of the meaning of the word."

"What *do* you tell them they need?"

"Christ. The person. Not the religion. Not the church. Not the denomination or any list of ethics. Our faith, true Christianity, is in the person of Jesus Christ. It's personal."

"OK, so you feel it's your duty, or you want to, or whatever, tell people about Christ. And you believe everyone needs it. Even if that's true, you know what's wrong with it? It's not as personal as you say it is."

"I don't follow."

"You tell me it's personal," she said. "And then you tell me that everyone needs it. If you make Earl Haymeyer feel like 'Everyman,' or like he should want and need this because everyone does, you can forget it."

"Keep going."

"If it's true that everyone needs Christ, and also that what they need is a person and not a religion or a church, then it *is* personal like you say. So you've got a dichotomy, and that's why it's so hard for you to speak coherently about it."

"You noticed?"

"Well, it's a tough one. Think of yourself as a marketing manager. You've got to sell widgets to everyone in the United States because your bosses have convinced you—and you believe them—that everyone not only could use a widget, but needs one. In fact, if they don't buy them, they'll regret it and you'll blame yourself for not selling them one."

"I'm with you so far."

"The only problem is, your market, that choice selection of buyers who all—and I mean one hundred percent, just like you've said—need widgets, don't know it."

"Don't know what?"

"That they need widgets."

"But you said I was convinced they needed them."

"Right, *you* are. *They* aren't. And what's worse, and what makes your job even tougher, is that you can't just advertise and convince everyone they need widgets. You know why? You've already hinted at it in your own example of the difference between Margo and the person who wants Christ in order to avoid hell."

"Tell me."

"They all need widgets for different reasons. You can't just barge in and say you need this because everyone needs it. That's what will make it an intrusion or condescending, like I said. It's your job to find out what need the widget will fill."

"But I still have to make the prospect aware of that need."

"Sure, but when you've taken the time to determine it, and you're right, he'll know you are right."

"And be more likely to respond to what I have to offer."

Hilary smiled and reached over to pat me on the head. "Even if it's true that everyone needs Christ to avoid hell, but you're going to reach them by showing them how He meets their *realized* needs."

113

Chapter Fourteen

Hilary and I had talked ourselves out. As we rolled on through Nevada, pushing for Las Vegas, we fell silent. Hilary did no more reading, and when I glanced at her during my turns to drive, she was either sleeping or gazing at the mountains that rimmed the horizon on all four sides.

I knew her arguments had left out the indispensible work of the Holy Spirit in a person's life. It takes more than marketing strategy, advertising, convincing, and all that. And yet, she had made sense. She had opened my eyes to the reaction of the unbeliever to the sharing of a Christian. And I hoped she had heard what I was really trying to say, all the while she was helping me say it. It was obvious she wasn't ready to be pushed.

The next morning we concurred that the Las Vegas nightlife and traffic could be heard from the windows of our respective hotel rooms until early in the morning. And when we went to check out, people were still playing the slots in the lobby at 5:30 A.M. We were still very tired and regretted the decision to spend the night in

Vegas, but it did perk us up to think that we were less than a day's drive from Los Angeles.

I took the first shift at the wheel and Hilary asked, "Can I get back to my lousy novel, or are we going to solve all the problems of mankind again today?"

I laughed. "You helped me a lot yesterday. Thanks."

"I won't know what to say if you and Margo ever get through to Earl. I'll feel partly responsible."

"We'll give you all the credit."

"Don't you dare."

Because we had time, we didn't feel rushed to get to Los Angeles. We stopped one time more than necessary for a snack and postponed our phone calls until we were in our rooms in L.A. We arrived just after noon and hung around the hotel lobby for a while, waiting for clean rooms.

I called Earl. "Why didn't you call last night?" he asked.

"It was late when we got to Vegas and even later in Chicago. What's up?"

"This whole thing stinks, Philip. It's gotten out of our hands, and I don't like it. Chakaris told me about this guy Fenton's involvement. What does Hilary know about him? Is he some kind of a jerk or something? Who does he think he is, pulling a separate deal with the Franklins and not letting anyone else even in his own firm know about it? Let me talk to her."

Hilary and Earl set up a conference call while I helped the bellboy get us moved into our rooms. Several minutes later, my phone rang. Chakaris, at his home, was on; Hilary, in her room, was on.

"Hi to everyone," Earl said. "Let's run this thing down now. If anyone has heard from Margo since Philip's message at Ogaloski or wherever that was in Nebraska, say so."

Silence.

"Anybody heard from Hollis Fenton?"

Silence.

"Anybody with any ideas? Let's start with you, Amos."

"I go back a long way with Hollis. It doesn't seem logical to me that he would be involved in some sort of collusion with one of my clients, but since that much of it is obviously true, I'm afraid I wouldn't put anything past him."

"Philip," Earl cut in, "you know Margo better than any of us. Where do you think she is?"

"I have no idea, Earl. I really don't."

"You have to guess, kid. I'm serious. We have to play some hunches here. Would she simply have gone somewhere other than with you or back to Chicago on her own?"

"I'd have to guess no. It doesn't sound like her. She was a loner before I met her, but not since."

"Things have changed since you met her, Philip," Hilary said.

"Yeah, but for all practical purposes her mother has been dead to her for years. I don't think it would change how she reacts to me."

"Earl," Amos said, "are you suggesting that Hollis

might be with her for some reason, taking her somewhere?"

"I don't know, Amos. I don't know what else to think. I just don't like it. I think we ought to go under the assumption that Margo is in trouble, being threatened perhaps, held against her will. I know that's morbid and may have no basis, but we'd better cover the possibility just in case. Would that kind of a threat affect Hilary's negotiations with Mr. Franklin?"

"First of all, the question is academic, Earl," Amos said. "There's no way our firm will negotiate against itself. Hollis Fenton—whether he's still with us or not—was with us when he drew up the document that's causing all the trouble. It actually outdates a bona fide will that I drew up. If Hollis is representing Mr. Franklin, we'll insist that he find other counsel—or that Hollis leave our firm."

"Which he already may have," Hilary said. "So what's next, Earl? What do you want us to do?"

"Before you get into that, Earl," Amos said, "I need to tell Hilary that Margo's father is insisting that their meeting take place tonight at ten, not tomorrow morning."

"Why?"

"Didn't say. Just a scheduling problem. He was ready Thursday morning, and now he wants tonight rather than tomorrow. We'd better comply."

"Yes," Haymeyer said. "But demand first to know if they know where Margo is. You won't tolerate any games. Amos, can we say that the will is up in the air

118

until we're satisfied that Margo is safe and responding on her own?"

"Sure."

"Then that's what we want to do. Hilary, do whatever else you were going to do, but insist that he tell you anything he knows about Margo. OK?"

Everyone agreed and we hung up. Hilary and I decided on an early dinner so she would have time to study the document from Mr. Henley that had been waiting at the desk. She couldn't keep from reading it at dinner. We agreed to meet at nine for the forty-five minute drive to Mr. Franklin's office. In the meantime I tried to sleep. And didn't succeed.

All we needed was more driving. I was dressed up and less comfortable than on the previous two thousand plus miles. Hilary was dressed for work, much the way she had been when Margo and I met her, but even more conservatively, if possible. She was striking, but mostly she looked professional. She would be taking nothing from Mr. Franklin or his lawyer, Hollis Fenton or not.

"I want to call his office from the lobby of his building before we go up to see if I can get a reading on what or whom we will encounter."

"Surely he'll have representation," I said.

"You'd think so."

Mr. Franklin's consulting service office was on the sixteenth floor of a thirty-story building that was virtually closed this late at night. A security guard pointed Hilary and me to the pay phones in the spacious lobby. Franklin answered his own phone.

"Mr. Franklin, this is Hilary Brice of the Chakaris

firm. Philip Spence of the EH Detective Agency is with me. May we come up?"

Hilary hung up and said he had simply directed her to the proper elevator and didn't hint that anyone else was there. "We'll just have to be adaptable."

We didn't speak on the elevator. I stood with my hands thrust deep into my pockets with my suitcoat buttoned. Hilary stood straight with her leather attaché tucked under her arm. If she was nervous, she didn't let on. We watched the floor lights blink to sixteen and the car floated to a stop. The door opened.

And there stood Margo.

She smiled almost smugly, and I couldn't even form the obvious question. She answered it anyway.

"I've been to Pontiac," she said.

"Why? How?"

"I took the bus straight into Chicago, rented a car, and drove down. Why? Because of the questions you asked me about my mother's letters, and because of something Amos said the day Mother died."

"Good grief," Hilary said. "We have a lot to talk about, but first, does your father know you're here?"

"Yes."

"Does he know you were in Pontiac?"

"No."

"Do me a favor and don't say anything, anything at all, until you're alone with us later." We heard footsteps at the end of the hall. "Promise me, Margo. Please."

"Promise."

"You must be Hilary Brice," Mr. Franklin said. "And hello, Philip. Good to see you again."

120

He led us to his office and to chairs around a small table. "I wanted you to meet my fiancee, but this is a little late for her. We'd like you to join us for an early dinner tomorrow at four-thirty."

"That would be fine," Hilary said, obviously anxious to get down to business. "Is your lawyer here?"

"I have a confession to make," Mr. Franklin said. "I don't really have a lawyer out here. Mr. Fenton of your firm represented me—us—on this, and when you called I pretended to be a lawyer representing me."

Margo was shocked at the mention of Fenton's name in association with the new document.

"Why did you feel the need to do that?" Hilary asked.

"I haven't been able to reach Mr. Fenton, and I've always felt a little vulnerable in such situations without representation. You understand."

"No, but if you say so," Hilary said.

"I suppose you want to see this," Mr. Franklin added, pulling the original document from the breast pocket of his coat. Hilary compared it with her photocopy.

"Do you have the cancelled check that shows you paid Mrs. Franklin one hundred thousand dollars for the option on the estate as spelled out in this contract?"

"Of course. My fiancee said you would ask for it. I also have a cashier's check here for fifty thousand dollars made out to Margo. Do you have title and deed to the property? I know Mr. Chakaris represented Virginia and filed virtually all her important papers."

"Daddy, why did mother leave me the house in one will and then leave it to you in another?"

"Margo, please," Hilary said.

"No, let me answer. At first it bothered me to know what she had done to you, honey," he said. "In fact, it still does. But then I realized that her request for fifty thousand to go to you before I acquire the estate was meant to heal the wound of her nullifying the previous will. I don't know why she chose not to destroy that will. I paid handsomely for my option on the estate through the years and then in the lump sum to your mother. She needed funds right then, and this was merely a business transaction. You have a nice inheritance and I have an investment that paid off, although in a not entirely happy way."

Margo burst into tears. "That must have been during the time that Mother was associated with the syndicate," she said. Mr. Franklin looked ashen.

"I don't want my client saying anything more right now," Hilary said. "I want you to know that you will not be nullifying a million dollar bequest with a payment of fifty thousand dollars without a verdict in court."

Margo started to protest, but Hilary stared her down. "Please wait and talk to me later," she said firmly. "Mr. Franklin, we will be studying this carefully. I believe you intend your daughter no harm, but her counsel will not allow her to settle for five percent of what we feel she is entitled to. I recommend that you secure counsel or get hold of Mr. Fenton or do whatever you feel is necessary to represent your position."

Mr. Franklin was still shaken. He had never been the type to stand up to a strong personality in a woman. He merely nodded and stood. We left quickly.

"You didn't even kiss me when you saw me," Margo said in the elevator.

I held her close. "Well, I, uh, I didn't exactly expect to—"

"I know," she said. "Have I got news for you two."

Chapter Fifteen

"Let's save it for the hotel, Margo," Hilary said. "I want to be able to take notes and get it all. Anyway, we need to let your friends in Chicago know you're still in the land of the living."

On our way back, Hilary told Margo of Hollis Fenton's secret involvement. At the hotel Hilary registered Margo to share her room, then we all met in mine where Hilary reported on the meeting in a late call to Chicago. Mr. Henley was waiting up for it.

"OK, Margo," Hilary said when she hung up. "Shoot. What've you got?"

"First let me tell you why I wanted to go to Pontiac," Margo began. "I had been in shock the last time I was there and hardly remembered anything about it. I found it difficult to believe my mother had actually been locked up in that place. The only time I'd been inside the front gate was the day she died. I just wanted to go back.

"And I wanted every memory to return. I wanted to remember the phone conversation I had with the woman doctor the night before Mother died. And I wanted to reread her letters and scrutinize everything. I'm glad I did. I also wanted to investigate something Amos said just before I saw Mother's body."

"What was that?" I said. "He said a lot of things."

"He said he didn't know the coroner, that he wasn't the one from Pontiac who usually served the prison there. Remember that?"

"Barely. But so what?"

"I got the coroner's name from the death certificate and discovered he was from Park Ridge. The Pontiac coroner didn't even hear of the death until a week later. The guy from Park Ridge said he was called the night before and was asked to be there the next morning. Mother died at four-thirty A.M."

Hilary looked puzzled. "It does sound strange, Margo," she said. "But of course it doesn't prove anything. You're insinuating that someone in the prison had a premonition about your mother's death, or that someone was going to die?"

"Let me finish and then I'll tell you what I'm insinuating. The woman in charge of food service told me that only prisoners in solitary confinement are segregated from the others during meals. Prisoners normally segregated from social, recreational, and work functions have their meals in the cafeteria, separated from the other women by only about twenty feet of floor space."

"So?"

"So Mother talked about having meals in her cell. And having chicken for what seemed to her like every meal."

"Maybe she had been restricted to her cell for illness or disciplinary reasons," Hilary said.

"I checked all that. Don't you see? I demanded to see reports and log sheets. The people in charge didn't think I was looking for anything in particular."

"So what did you find?"

"I found that chicken was not served to any prisoner during the week Mother wrote about it. Not to the general population, nor to any prisoner in solitary or restricted confinement."

"Could your mother have been mistaken? You said she had been ill or out of sorts."

"No! She was not one to miss details, and she certainly knew when she was eating chicken! She wasn't dizzy or disoriented until she had eaten the chicken a few times. The chicken that it seems only she was served."

"What are you saying, Margo?" Hilary asked. "Exactly what are you implying?"

"That my mother was poisoned."

Hilary shook her head impatiently. "It would have shown up on the autopsy."

"Not if whoever poisoned her owns the coroner."

Hilary set her pen on her steno pad and entwined her long fingers. She stared at Margo, who seemed on the verge of crying again. "You don't want to know who is implicated first if there's anything to this," Hilary said.

"I know. Daddy. But of course he could not be guilty. We all know that."

"Yeah," I said.

"Well, not *all* of us know that," Hilary said. "He has a motive."

"For killing Mother? Never."

"His motive is the estate. The house. A little payment to keep you happy, and everything is his."

"That's not enough of a motive for Daddy. Why wouldn't he have killed her before? Anytime after the document had been signed?"

"It might have looked too obvious. This was convenient. How could a man in California get into an Illinois prison to do in his ex-wife? It was a perfect setup to make him look innocent."

"No way," I said. "I have to agree with Margo, Hilary, and I don't think I'm being naive. I believe that man loved his wife even to her death. He didn't need her million dollar estate. It doesn't add up, even though things look bad for him."

"The story is far-fetched anyway," Hilary said, paging through her notes. "It doesn't make sense that the prison officials were that free with their time and log sheets. Why would they show them to *you*?"

"Because I played the little-girl-lost bit to the hilt. And I was good. I didn't lie or cheat to get to see any of it. I just begged. I wanted to see some evidence of her last days. She never told me anything about a cold, yet her infirmary reports say she was heavily medicated against the symptoms."

"Maybe they showed you what they wanted you to see," Hilary said. "Another autopsy could prove what you're saying, one way or the other. Do you want us to petition to have the body exhumed?"

Margo grimaced. "Ooh," she said. "I don't know about that."

We sat in silence for a few moments before Hilary spoke. "Let me tell you something straight. I think this is all off the wall. Your mother simply didn't tell you about some of these details because she was upset or didn't think of them or didn't want to worry you. Your allegations are going to be hard to prove, and if they do pan out, the finger is going to point straight at the man with the motive, your father. Since he is just a few semester hours from canonization in both of your minds, you obviously don't want to see him face charges. So what have you got? You've got a situation you don't want."

"I'm telling you my mother was poisoned to death. I want to know who did it."

"If you are convinced your father is clean, you'd better come up with someone with a motive. Who would stand to gain by your mother's death? Someone with the influence to buy a doctor, a coroner, an autopsy, and a few bit part players."

"Think of the initials on that new document," I said, "and you've answered your own question."

"Fenton? Nah! Why would Fenton care? What would he have to gain? His percentage of the estate would hardly be worth the risk, unless he was getting a significant share of the gross."

"We've got to get hold of Earl," I said, dialing his office in Glencoe. I got the answering device. I rang Bonnie's apartment, forgetting how late it was in Chicago.

"I'm sorry to wake you, but I've got to get a message to Earl. Know where I can reach him?"

"Not really; he's on the move. Calls in every morning, though. Shall I tell him it's urgent?"

"It's more than urgent, Bon. He needs to call me from wherever he is as soon as he can. Tell him anything you have to, to get him to call me. I'll wait by the phone."

We ordered a snack from room service before the girls went to their room. Then I called Margo. "I haven't even told you how much I missed you and worried about you," I said. "Why didn't you tell me where you were?"

"I was afraid you'd want me to stay in Glencoe. I needed to do this, Philip."

"How in the world did you beat us out here?"

"Once I had my information, I took a bus. They don't stop for sleep, you know. They just change drivers."

"How are you feeling about all this?"

"As you'd imagine. I thought I was all through with it. All I know is that Daddy is innocent. How Hollis Fenton would get any of the money is beyond me. If Daddy thought Mr. Fenton had anything to do with Mother's death, he wouldn't have anything to do with him. And he surely wouldn't give him any money."

"Of course not," I agreed. But I fell asleep as puzzled as she.

The phone woke me at 5:00 A.M. I knew it had to be Earl.

"Where are you?" I asked groggily.

"Springfield, Illinois," he said. "A conference and some business. What's up? Bonnie said it was more than urgent."

I told him the whole story.

Chapter Sixteen

"One major problem," Earl said. "Unless Margo was lucky, she simply got her chain pulled in Pontiac. I just can't see anyone there giving her anything legit, especially if there *was* any collusion by insiders."

"Do you think it's possible there was, Earl?"

"Anything is possible in that Franklin family. The poor woman couldn't even get to her grave in peace."

"Not many people do."

"I know. I know."

"What do you think? What can we do?"

"Well, for one thing, I want to get to Pontiac and see if I can corroborate anything Margo learned. I'll see if I can get Amos to meet me there, because he knows Hollis Fenton better than anyone. The thing I can't get to add up is Mr. Franklin's role. He just isn't the type of a guy who would have his former wife killed just to get her money. He doesn't need it, and he doesn't hold grudges. I've been in the business long enough that I shouldn't be fooled. I've seen apparent weaklings murder two or three people, but George Franklin isn't that type of bird."

"That's what Margo and I have been saying. Listen, do you really have time to go to Pontiac?"

"No, but I'll just forget this conference for now. Other business will have to wait. You and Margo are getting to be like family, and that makes you priorities."

"We appreciate that, Earl. But I feel badly about it. I should be doing the legwork on this."

"You are, Philip, but you can't be in two places at once. Good thing that air traffic controllers' strike was settled. Maybe I can get a small plane out of here this morning for some dirt road landing strip near Pontiac."

"I didn't even know the strike was over."

"That means you're doing your job. I'll call you as soon as I have something. What's your schedule today?"

"We're just meeting Mr. Franklin and his fiancee for an early dinner at four-thirty this afternoon. Between now and then, we don't know what to do."

"You'd better sit tight. I'll be getting back to you. Hilary will have a tough time holding off Mr. Franklin without a formal injunction against what appears to be his legal right to acquire the estate."

I rang Hilary's room. Margo answered.

"Sorry to wake you. Let me talk to Hilary."

"No, you don't. I'm the one who tracked down all the information. I want to be in on this. I'm not gonna sit by while everyone else decides my fate, like last time."

I told her Earl's plans. Meanwhile, Hilary stirred and tried to listen with Margo. "This is silly," she finally broke in. "Meet us for breakfast downstairs in a half hour."

"What if Earl calls?"

"He won't even be out of Springfield in a half hour,"

she said. "Anyway, we can be reached in the coffee shop here."

I'm sure I looked as bleary-eyed as the girls did, but breakfast woke me up. "Earl seems to think there's a missing link," I said. "He wants to find the connection between Hollis Fenton and your father."

"Somehow it's hard to imagine your father being totally unaware of anything underhanded in your mother's death, especially when he stands to gain so much," Hilary said.

"You don't know him," Margo said. "He didn't know she was seeing Richard Wanmacher either. I maintain that he is—just as you say—totally unaware. I wonder how he'd react if I played my hunch and told him I didn't want any money."

"I've been thinking about that too," Hilary said. "We need some kind of a lead on how Hollis Fenton thinks he's going to get his fingers into this pie. Unless he's getting a major share somehow, why would this all be worth it? Margo, why don't you see what you can find out? If you make noise like you're going to make it easy for them, maybe it'll flush them out."

Margo called her father from her room while Hilary and I remained in the restaurant. "What do you think she's going to find?" I asked.

"I don't know. I still think her father is just after the money, but you two are pretty convincing." Margo returned in about twenty minutes.

"Daddy says Hollis Fenton is flying out here today and will be at our dinner this afternoon."

Hilary's eyes lit up. "Amos wouldn't want me contesting another lawyer within our firm, but Amos isn't really my boss anymore. And Fenton may not be with our firm anymore either."

"I learned something else," Margo said. "His new woman has a lot of influence."

"I caught that last night," Hilary said. "When he said she told him I would want to see the cancelled check. How would she know that? She sounds pretty sharp. Unless she's a lawyer."

"I don't think she's a lawyer," Margo said, "but every time I asked Daddy a question about the document or the estate, he told me what she said and how she felt and what she advised. It's almost as if she wants this deal more than he does. They're both very anxious for me to just take the money, whether I want it or not."

"You think she's got him to commit part of his estate—which would include the inheritance if this is consummated—to her upon their marriage?" Hilary said.

"I've never heard of that," Margo said. "Would he be bound by it?"

"You bet he would, especially in this state. Then she just finds quick grounds for divorce and makes off with whatever percentage of his estate she's legally entitled to."

"And that's legal?"

"It happens every day, Margo," Hilary said.

"You're not saying that Mr. Franklin's fiance had something to do with Mrs. Franklin's death, are you?" I said. "This is getting pretty wild."

134

"I don't know," Hilary said. "If she didn't have anything to do with it, she sure came along at a strategic moment in his life, didn't she?"

"I'd really like to meet this woman," Margo said.

"No, you wouldn't," I said. "I wasn't going to tell you, but she was the real reason your father didn't come back for the funeral."

"You said he said it was because of the air traffic strike."

"That's what he told me to say. But really, it was this Gertrude or Gilda—"

"Gladys," Margo corrected.

Hilary wrote it down. "Gladys what?" she said.

"Turner, I think. Do you remember, Philip?"

"No."

"When Earl calls again," Hilary said, "let me talk to him."

"You mean you don't think I'm an astute enough private investigator to pick up on the fact that he and Amos ought to try to check out this woman too?"

"You didn't remember her name, Philip," Hilary said.

"I do remember Margo saying Gladys was a transplanted Chicagoan."

"That's a big help. I'm sure any number of Chicagoans would know her, then, wouldn't they?"

"Why are you being sarcastic, Hilary?" I said. "I'm just trying to help."

"I'm just teasing, Philip. But saying she's from Chicago is like saying that your father was in World War Two and might have known my father."

"He was."

"Was what?"

"Was in World War Two. Was your father too, really?"

"Honestly, Philip. Yes, he was. Stationed in Iwo Jima."

"You're kidding! So was mine!" I said. "What year?"

"Starting in nineteen forty-two."

"I don't believe this! I'll give you my father's name, and you check it out with your dad, OK?"

"You can't be serious, Philip."

"Of course I'm not serious. We can both tease, can't we? My father was a camp clerk, stateside."

Hilary shook her head. "I must keep reminding myself that we're adults," she said.

"Mr. Spence?" the waitress said. "There's a phone call for you."

"May I take it in my room?"

"Surely. I'll have it transferred."

We paid quickly and ran for the elevators.

Earl told me he had reached Pontiac and was having more luck than he had hoped for because of the weekend staff on duty. "They're anxious to prove they know what's going on. Virtually everything Margo found is being substantiated. I talked to the Park Ridge pathologist. I think he's clean. He said he got a call the night before from a doctor down here, asking if he would perform an autopsy the next day because the Pontiac man was going to be off.

136

"I asked him if he thought it was a strange request, but he said he had been to Pontiac occasionally on other cases, so he didn't think too much about it."

"Earl," I interrupted, "what time of the night was he called?"

"Late. About eleven."

"Margo talked to a doctor in the prison not long before that. Why wasn't she told anything about her mother's condition if it was bad enough to alert a coroner? And didn't you and Amos tell us that Mrs. Franklin died early in the morning?"

"The report shows that she was discovered dead in her infirmary bed at four-thirty A.M.," Margo cued me. I told Earl.

"I reminded him of that," Earl said. "It was also on the death certificate. He said he had noticed that but assumed it was an insignificant clerical error and didn't mention it to anyone at the prison. His only other hangup with the case was that the doctor had told him of a cold, which he couldn't verify through the autopsy. The only problem he found was traces of a gastric condition that could have been brought on by something she ate. Not enough to hurt her, he said, but enough to get her into the infirmary. He feels a minor cold, hardly traceable, *could* have killed her because her heart did appear to have been in a weakened condition.

"When I was convinced that he might have been an unwitting accomplice, I asked him if there was any way Mrs. Franklin could have been murdered without his detecting it. He said there were many ways, but that since he went into the autopsy without any suspicions, it

137

was routine. He based his search on the doctor's prognosis and found everything in order. At the time he had little reason to believe that she had not died, as the doctor said, as the result of low resistance to a heart attack, due to a minor cold. A more complete autopsy would have had to have been warranted in advance."

I asked Earl to wait a minute and tried to relay the conversation to Margo and Hilary. "I want the body exhumed," Hilary said flatly. I told Earl. Margo made a face.

"I'll mention it to Amos," Earl said. "He'll know how to get it done. He should be here any time."

Chapter Seventeen

At about one o'clock Los Angeles time, Earl called again. "We have a court order to have the body exhumed, but it can't be done until Monday morning. Meanwhile, you want to guess how many Gladys Turners there have been in Chicago? Thousands, and many of them with records. You need to get a good look at this woman and get some more information out of her. Is it possible the reason she didn't meet you last night was because she wanted to find out who all was there before she showed her face?"

"Why would she do that?"

"I don't know. It just seems strange that she wouldn't meet her future step-daughter the first chance she got. And maybe there's someone she wants to avoid."

"We'll be seeing her this afternoon. Hollis Fenton will be there, too."

That was news to Earl, and he knew it would be to Amos too. He covered the phone and told him. When he came back on, I could hear the old man fuming in the background. "I don't think I'm going to be able to talk Amos out of coming out there," Earl said. "He's hot. He's heard nothing from Hollis since he stormed out several days ago. If I finish my investigation here, I may come out with him. A little surprise meeting between Amos and Hollis might not be a bad idea.''

I asked Hilary where we were supposed to meet Mr. Franklin, Miss Turner, and Mr. Fenton. She took the phone. "At the Pub Club on Ventura Boulevard, Earl, but tell Amos I was kinda looking forward to confronting Fenton myself. It'll feel good to outlawyer him, no tricks . . . Oh, good. That'll be great.''

She hung up and told us that Earl and Amos wanted us to delay the meeting until seven and they promised not to drop in on us until about eight. "Meanwhile," she said, "it's strategy time.''

We spent the rest of the afternoon trading theories, wondering whether Gladys Turner was involved, whether Mr. Franklin was totally in the dark as usual, how he and Miss Turner had met, and just what we were supposed to get out of her that would help Earl put the pieces together. I would have liked to put them all together myself, but by now I was totally confused. I wondered if this business ever got easier.

Mr. Franklin had no problem with postponing the dinner a few hours, though he sounded a bit puzzled. The time dragged.

That evening Miss Turner was a surprise to all of us. She was of average height but was unusually thin and mousy looking. Her hair was made up in a ratted style from years ago, and she wore orange-tinted glasses. She was, however, dressed expensively.

"Hollis will be here shortly," Mr. Franklin said more

than once, and he continually looked over our heads and behind us to watch for him.

Hilary tried to keep things social until Hollis arrived, and I knew she was hoping he would come before Amos and Earl showed up. The later it got, the more we wondered whether Earl had finished his work and if they were able to get a flight, knowing most would be fully booked after the lengthy strike.

Miss Turner, however, wanted to get on with business. "Exactly what do you have in mind, Miss Brice, that will stop this transaction?"

"I prefer to wait until Mr. Franklin's counsel arrives, if you don't mind."

"I do mind, but I don't suppose I'm going to change yours."

Hilary tried to kill the hard woman with kindness. "Let's talk about you, Miss Turner. Margo tells us you're a native Chicagoan."

"And how did you know that?" Gladys said, staring at Margo.

"Isn't that what you told me, Daddy?"

"Yes, but, you see, Gladys has less than happy memories from Chicago. She'd rather talk about Los Angeles."

Gladys's thin face broke into a reluctant smile, and she tucked her arm beneath Mr. Franklin's, though her body remained rigid.

"Here's Hollis now." Mr. Franklin beamed, rising as if to meet his salvation from an awkward situation.

Fenton was loaded for bear, smelling right, looking right, wearing the right clothes and jewelry, and even carrying the right portfolio. He was the epitome of the man in charge, and Mr. Franklin and I immediately deferred to his presence. Hilary, however, all but arched her back.

As he had been the first time we had seen him, Hollis Fenton was as smooth as silk. "George, it's good to see you again. Hello, Hilary, Margo, Philip, and this must be your intended. Why, Miss, uh, Turner, you're even more lovely than George said. The pleasure is all mine."

Miss Turner looked embarrassed and said nothing. I nearly gagged. Saying she was lovely was an insult to Hilary and all the other women he had ever made passes at, probably including the late Mrs. Franklin. "Are you ready to talk business, Mr. Fenton?" Hilary asked.

"Oh, my dear, let's eat first. I'm starved. This was originally scheduled for much earlier, and I haven't eaten." He signaled the waiter, ordered drinks all around, then grinned broadly as Hilary and Margo and I declined. "Then we'll have the best steaks in the house," he said, "and you may bring me the bill."

"I don't care for steak," Hilary told the waiter politely. "I suggest your taking our orders individually, and I will be paying for the three of us."

Mr. Franklin, Miss Turner, and Mr. Fenton ordered steaks. I wanted to as well, but I was getting into Hilary's nonviolent resistance, so I ordered roast beef. Hilary and Margo ordered fish.

Hilary smiled sweetly at Hollis. "Will both these bills be on Chakaris, Fenton, Henley, and Whitehead, or should I say Henley, Whitehead, Fenton, and Chakaris?"

142

"As a matter of fact, you shouldn't say either," Hollis said. "The firm of Fenton and Fenton will move into offices right here in Los Angeles in a few days."

"How nice for you. And for your son, I presume?"

"Yes, my youngest. He came with a real price tag, but he'll be worth it."

Hollis rambled on about his son and the new firm while we ate. Hilary was stony, but she appeared ready for battle. As dessert was served, she tore into Fenton. There was no buildup.

"Don't you think it looks a little strange that you and Mr. Franklin have a secret agreement, secret even from one of the principals—Margo here—and from the very firm you represented at the time you drew up the papers?"

"That was the wish of my client, dear. I cannot violate the wishes of my client."

"And who was your client? Mr. Franklin or Mrs. Franklin?"

"In this case, Mr. But she needed the money and he wanted a good investment."

"And what do *you* get out of this?"

"A percentage, you know that. We all know that. The deal is perfectly legal, and if you have no bona fide reasons we shouldn't complete the transaction immediately, I suggest you comply or face legal charges yourself."

"Don't be silly, counselor," Hilary said. "A lawyer who would violate the ethics of his own profession is a lawyer whose every move should be scrutinized, especially one who would stiff his own partners."

"In an archaic firm, at that," Fenton said. "And what will you gain by scrutinizing me? You know our document takes precedence on the basis of date alone, and there's nothing whatever illegal about it, despite the irregularities the client's confidence required."

"Excuse me, Hollis," Mr. Franklin broke in, "but are you saying that this contract was not known to others at your law firm?"

"George, let me handle this. Your former wife was embarrassed to be acquiring such a lump sum and simply asked that I—as an old friend and colleague—not tell Amos about it. It had to be filed separately because *he* had drawn up the last previous will."

Mr. Franklin still looked puzzled, but Hollis tried to ignore him.

"You said George was your client," Hilary pressed. "Why follow the wishes of Mrs. Franklin when you represented Mr. Franklin?"

"And wasn't Mrs. Franklin more than an old friend and colleague?" I asked.

"What are you talking about?" Fenton said, flushing. "And why are *you* talking anyway? This is none of your business."

"Hollis, let's get back to business," Hilary said.

"Yes, let's," he said, louder than before. "I have a right to know exactly how you're going to try to stop this transaction. We have a check cut for Margo, and I trust you have the title and deed to the property."

"No, we don't. And you can *keep* your check. Quite frankly, we have serious questions regarding Mrs. Franklin's death."

"You saw the body. You know she's dead. What more do you want?"

"We want to know how she died."

Mr. Franklin looked as if someone had punched him in the stomach.

Hollis Fenton spoke. "You know how she died if you talked with the attending physician and the coroner. It's all on record. I even have copies of everything with me. Don't you?"

"Of course I do. I just don't like it. I don't like the fact that Mr. Franklin's fiancee came into his life not long before he was to come into a million dollars."

Miss Turner bristled. Hilary charged on. "I'd be very interested to know if there isn't a prenuptial financial agreement between Miss Turner and Mr. Franklin that includes the very estate we're talking about."

Mr. Franklin looked at Hollis, who jumped in quickly. "That is totally irrelevant, and you know there would be no way for you to petition to see it. It would have no bearing, even if it existed."

"Which it does," Mr. Franklin said.

"George," Hollis said.

"But I'm proud of it. Gladys was jilted once and taken for all her savings another time. I am perfectly willing to assure her, legally, that the same thing will not happen again. She's protected should we divorce, but we will not be divorcing."

"Uh-huh," Hilary said, unconvinced.

"The details of any such document are irrelevant to this discussion. Even if we produced such an agreement, it would prove nothing. Miss Turner is practical and Mr.

145

Franklin is generous. I, for one, think we need more of that in this country."

"Oh, shut up," Hilary said. "Honestly, Hollis, you sit here spouting like a Boy Scout after you've set this woman up for life at your client's expense—"

"Now wait a minute," George Franklin said. "If you're suggesting—"

"I'm suggesting, Mr. Franklin, that you've been had. Don't you think it a little unusual that you meet this woman, she takes an inordinate interest in you to the point of your falling in love with her, she tells you stories about her sad past that make you anxious to promise her anything, your promises are then legally contracted for by the lawyer who also encouraged you to take advantage of your former wife under the guise of helping her, and now you find that he never told anyone, not even his partners, about that contract? Does that not arouse any suspicion in your mind?"

"Ignore her, George," Hollis said. "She's just trying to get her client more than she's entitled to."

"Her client happens to be my daughter, Hollis," George said. "If Virginia intended to leave her the house, then perhaps she's entitled to it. I don't want to fight my own daughter for money or property or anything else. And Gladys, you *have* been pushing me to do just that. Both of you have. I trust you, but I'm going to need time to think."

"You'll have plenty of time," Hilary said. "We're going to do everything we can to slow the paperwork on your contract with Mrs. Franklin, and if I were you, I'd get the processing halted on your agreement with your fiancee too."

Gladys glared at him. "If you hold up that paperwork," she said, "it'll be the end of us."

"Gladys," Mr. Franklin whined. "This doesn't sound like you."

"After all I've been through," she said. "I could never trust another man."

Mr. Franklin put his arm around her. "All right," he said softly. "All right."

"While we're on the subject, Mr. Franklin, how would you feel if you knew your former wife was murdered?" Hilary said.

He could hardly comprehend her words.

Hollis squinted at her and shook his head. "What in the world are you trying to do?" he said.

Hilary ignored him and kept talking to George. "How long after Gladys came into your life did Mrs. Franklin die? How long after you promised her half your estate?"

"Enough of this," Hollis said. "You don't have to listen—either of you. It's ridiculous."

"Well, look who's here," Hilary said cheerfully as Amos and Earl approached. Fenton closed his eyes and opened them slowly. George Franklin tried to smile. Gladys Turner put her hand to her mouth and looked down.

Chapter Eighteen

As two extra chairs were squeezed around the table, tense introductions were made and Hollis Fenton fought to maintain his composure. He asked through pursed lips to what he owed "the pleasure of this surprise?"

"My office—or my former office anyway—tells me that your resignation arrived in the mail this morning," Chakaris said. "Nice of you to have it come on a Saturday when only a few people were there."

"Well, I don't know if you've had a chance to see it or read it yet, boss, but it simply reiterates what I've felt all along: that working for you was a highlight, a challenge, and a privilege, and that I had to move on to get my name first on a firm's stationery."

"And we both know that's baloney, don't we, ol' friend? You've been on the ropes for the last several years, and you couldn't face me or the other partners with your final decision, which we would have eventually come to as well. You saved the partners a difficult task."

"So that's why you're here? To face me? To tell me good-bye? To tell me that I didn't give enough notice?"

"Well, the latter is true enough, isn't it? I mean, we're not the local factory with a line of welders waiting to get in and take over, are we? Your contract calls for ninety days notice and your assistance in screening junior partners to replace you."

"But that's not why you're here."

"Nope. We just want to listen in."

Hilary tried to recap the conversation, with Hollis interrupting with rebuttals and corrections every few sentences. But Amos was not looking at either of them. He may have been listening, but he was staring at Miss Turner. Occasionally she would peek up at him, only to lower her eyes again. Her hand still covered her mouth, though not as if she were startled, as when they had first arrived. She was simply sitting there with her left elbow on the table and her chin and mouth buried in her left palm.

Chakaris, whose voice can be as big as he is when he wants it to be, cut off Fenton's and Hilary's arguments by speaking over them to Gladys. "So, tell me about yourself," he said.

She cocked her head and looked at him, but kept her hand where it was. She pulled back a fraction so he could hear her past her cupped hand, and when she had spoken, she settled back into her former position. "Not much to tell," she said. "Sort of a nobody from nowhere."

"Oh, nonsense," Chakaris said. "Everybody's somebody and everybody's from somewhere. Where've you lived, what've you done, who are you? C'mon, it takes an impressive woman to land a guy like George here.

150

Surely he wouldn't be interested in a shy girl who won't even show her face."

Gladys smiled self-consciously and tucked her chin between her thumb and forefinger so he had a slightly better look at her. She answered his questions with monosyllables. "Is Mr. Fenton your lawyer too?" Amos asked.

"Not really," she said.

"As a matter of fact," Hollis cut in, "I worked up the papers between Mr. Franklin and Miss Turner without ever having met her. It was his idea. He knew of her bad experiences in the past and insisted upon protecting her legally. I had not met her until tonight myself. She's not the type of a woman who would procure a lawyer to challenge her own husband-to-be."

"No, I'm sure she's not," Chakaris said, smiling fatherly at her.

Chakaris had not taken his eyes off the woman for several minutes. Fenton kept asking if anything was going to be accomplished or resolved and if not, could he schedule a later meeting.

"No, sir," Chakaris said evenly, his eyes still locked in on Gladys. "I want to clear this up tonight. Do you know that a judge is sitting in my former office right now, sipping my coffee and maybe even sampling a little of Mr. Henley's Scotch? You remember Mr. Henley, Hol, the guy who got the position you wanted so badly? The judge won't get himself drunk tonight, though. He never does. Especially when he's working weekends and has already given an order to have a body exhumed.

"He works on weekends only for old, old, friends.

And even then he'll only do it when he can help those friends nail a rat."

"You're talking in circles, Amos," Fenton said. "And if you don't mind my saying so, you're being extremely rude to Miss Turner. I believe you're embarrassing the lady by staring at her so."

"Well, Hollis, I'm not talking in circles. I do have a judge waiting for my call. I told him that even if I didn't run into anything new out here, I would still call him and tell him of all the circumstantial evidence we had run into. I didn't expect you to make it this easy for me, Hol. But then you and Gladys didn't expect to see me here tonight either."

Amos waved to the maitre d' who brought a phone to our table. "And no, I don't mind your saying that I'm being rude to Miss Turner. Perhaps I am. But this lady, as you call her, is no Miss Turner. Unless she's been married since her first husband died, this woman has been Mrs. John Margolis for two decades."

Gladys pressed both hands to her cheeks and slid them up to cover her eyes as her glasses rattled to the table. She inhaled deeply and her knuckles turned white against her face.

"Well, old John died a lot of years ago, and I haven't seen Gladys since then. But she was one of those old, old friends I was talking about. And they're hard to fool, aren't they, honey?"

Gladys nodded, but her face was still hidden.

"Hollis, my pal, I'm going to call my judge in Chicago now. And I'm going to finish the story I started to tell him just before we flew out here.

"I don't know how you got enough bad chicken into Mrs. Franklin to make her sick enough to get her into the infirmary. And I don't know how you got the Park Ridge pathologist to help you without arousing his suspicion. I probably won't know until Monday just what it took to kill Mrs. Franklin, but I think the judge will agree with me that a warrant for your arrest, and that of Gladys Margolis, is appropriate.

"I believe he has the California contacts to have you detained for extradition to Illinois to face charges for conspiracy to commit murder."

We sat stunned, listening, wondering. Hollis Fenton's breath came in great rushes through his nose as he kept his mouth tightly closed. Chakaris let a pregnant silence hang in the air as he put his big hand on the phone. Mr. Franklin finally spoke.

"Please, someone, tell me what's going on." He looked pleadingly at me and at Earl Haymeyer.

"Even I don't know, Amos," Earl said. "You might as well give us all of it."

"Would you like to tell it yourself, Gladys?" Chakaris asked softly.

She shook her head.

"The woman Hollis says is Gladys Turner," he explained, "is Gladys Margolis. And she used to work in our offices. She was Hollis Fenton's secretary, and she typed up the agreement between the Franklins."

Chakaris looked pityingly at his former partner. "All I needed was a connection between you and Mr. Franklin, something that would justify your taking such an interest in his estate."

153

"I didn't want any part of this, Amos," Gladys said through tears. "He said it would be so easy, and that I wouldn't have to have anything to do with the murder. We were going to split the money after I got it from George. I've had a rough time since John died, Amos. I never got a break. Hollis said we could pull it off once you had retired and George moved to California."

"I wonder, Gladys," Amos said, "given the sad man Hollis is, how long you suppose he would have let you keep your half?"

"Gladys," George Franklin managed, just above a whisper. "I thought you loved me. I loved you."

"That was the sickest thing about this, and about you," she said with contempt. "Getting next to you was the easiest job I ever had."

Late that night, in Mr. Franklin's spacious apartment, Amos Chakaris sympathetically told George and Margo how he had hated to expose Gladys in front of everyone. "Giving Hollis his due didn't bother me a bit, but Gladys *has* had her share of rough breaks. Nothing that would justify what she's been party to, but rough nonetheless.

"I recognized something about her immediately, but I couldn't put my finger on it, and it *has* been a lot of years. I can't tell you how shocked I was when I realized who she was. When it became obvious that she was hiding from me, I just stared her down and racked my brain. When she spoke the second or third time, it all came back to me."

Amos asked to use the phone, and when he had left

the room, Mr. Franklin said, "I feel like a fool. I've been made the fool so many times it's a wonder I can function as an adult. How can I be so gullible?"

"It's a hazard of your sweet nature," Margo said, but he didn't appear consoled. "Maybe you need me out here for a while to protect you and take care of you."

I rolled my eyes.

"I couldn't let you do that, Margo," he said. "One of these days you've got to start living your own life."

"So far 'my own life' has been horrible," she said. "Next I'll hear that someone is trying to kill you or Philip."

"There's a lesson in this for all of us," I said, immediately realizing how sermonic I sounded. It seemed everyone was looking at me with utmost toleration. "At least it was a lesson for me," I added weakly.

And it had been. There was no way Margo could argue with that. She had been concerned about her mother and now her father, and we had both hoped for opportunities to tell Haymeyer about Christ. Hilary knew where we were coming from spiritually, and our work with her was cut out for us. With the kind of business we were getting into and the undeniably strange family Margo had come from, no one knew what could happen to any one of us next.

I wanted to tell Margo that we needed to plan and work and pray about sharing our faith with our friends, but this wasn't the time. At least it didn't seem the time to me. But she surprised me.

"Philip's right," she said, coming to my defense,

albeit not as quickly as I might have hoped. "I'm still in shock over Mother's death and what Daddy has gone through, but I don't feel like retreating and sleeping it off or running and hiding from it. I just feel like you never know how much time you have to tell the people close to you what's really important to you."

"Are we gonna get the whole pitch right here tonight, Margo?" Haymeyer asked.

"Only if you want it," she said.

"Not really."

"Your time is coming, Earl," she said with a smile.

"I know that. I was impressed with your work in Pontiac, and I'm anxious to have you working with me and getting back on the waiting list for detective school."

Amos returned from the phone to report that two arrests at the women's facility in Pontiac had already led to confessions and direct implications of Hollis Fenton. He pulled me aside. "Tell Margo if she wants to know and when you feel she's up to it: her mother was killed by an injection of air into the bloodstream. Almost impossible to detect through autopsy, but an orderly has confessed to it."

Hollis Fenton and Gladys Margolis would be found as guilty as the pair they paid to do the dirty work.

With the air strike over, we left the rented car and flew back together. All I could think of was that Margo had wanted to work with me so we could get to know each other better, predicting that all the problems we would face would belong to other people.

So far, she'd been wrong. Dead wrong. She could still call my love pity or sympathy. She could say our relationship was entrenched in trauma and crisis. And I couldn't argue.

All I could do was to stay close and hope she would realize that my love was constant, regardless of whether she was in trouble, in shock, or in mourning.

In Margo Mystery No. 4, *Paige,* Earl Haymeyer meets Paige, someone to care for after having lost his wife years ago. She's everything he ever could have hoped for and more, but why are people telling lies about her. What secrets from the past still haunt her?